I was alone in the d...

Rain rapped and drummed on the surface of our little Volvo. The fog had really rolled in, covering the ground in a thick cottony shroud. The view through the front window was like looking at a wet blackboard.

It was *mondo* creepy.

To take my mind off the situation, I started to go over the day's events. What had really happened back in the mall? Maybe Daddy was right. Maybe my brain *was* playing tricks on me.

Am I going crazy?

I shifted uncomfortably in my seat and tried not to think about it. Something was poking out of my skirt pocket. A piece of paper.

I unfolded it, holding it up to the window. I had to peer closely at it to make anything out in the gloom.

As if on cue, a brilliant lightning bolt flashed across the sky, illuminating the note. A strangely familiar handwriting came into sharp focus:

NO, YOU 'RE NOT CRAZY,
BUT YOU <u>ARE</u> IN DANGER

Alien Terror
Alien Blood
Alien Scream
Second Sight
Shape-shifter
Aftershock

Available from MINSTREL® Paperbacks

mindwarp ™

Aftershock

by

Chris Archer

A MINSTREL® BOOK

Published by POCKET BOOKS
New York   London   Toronto   Sydney   Tokyo   Singapore

*To Chrissy, Danielle, Ali, Marielle . . . and Bobby, who will have to
fend for himself.*

A MINSTREL PAPERBACK *Original*

A Minstrel Book published by
POCKET BOOKS, a division of Simon & Schuster Inc.
1230 Avenue of the Americas, New York, NY 10020

mindwarp™ is a trademark of Daniel Weiss Associates, Inc.
Produced by Daniel Weiss Associates, Inc., New York

Copyright © 1998 by Daniel Weiss Associates, Inc.
Cover art copyright © 1998 by Daniel Weiss Associates, Inc.

ISBN: 0-671-01487-0

First Minstrel Books printing June 1998

10 9 8 7 6 5 4 3 2 1

A MINSTREL BOOK and colophon are registered trademarks of
Simon & Schuster Inc.

Printed in the U.S.A.

Chapter 1

I stared my opponent straight in the eye. She was a good two heads taller than me, but I knew I could take her. I was younger. Quicker. And I'd come to the battle prepared.

She was going *down*.

My name is Toni Douglas, and if there's one thing I've learned, it's that attitude is everything. My attitude at this moment was, Surrender the Goods.

For reinforcement I glanced down at the words I had written on my pocket notepad and day planner:

TRIUMPH. CONQUEST. VICTORY. NO MERCY.

Harsh words, but after all, shopping is war.

I ran a hand through my long brown hair and

flashed my most radiant smile. "But is it on sale?" I persisted. "And if it isn't on sale now, will it be on sale next week?"

The saleslady, whose name tag read *Meredith* in tiny gold letters, didn't even flinch. Instead she tossed back her head with a little laugh.

Yes, you heard right. She was laughing at me, adorable me, sweet me, extremely-bad-idea-to-laugh-at me.

"Sale?" she scoffed. "Little girl, this is *haute couture*. This blouse is one of a kind. It has been shown in the summer collection at Paris, London, and Milan. If you can't afford it, you can't afford it, and if you can't afford it, you can't wear it. End of story."

You may be wondering to yourself where they found such snotty people in a little town like Metier, Wisconsin, where I have lived all of my thirteen fabulous years. *I* certainly was wondering. My theory is that the owners of Boutique Chic imported them directly from Paris, where they have special schools for salesladies that teach you how to sneer and speak with a French accent at the same time.

Any other day I might have turned around and walked right out. But today was different. Today I wasn't shopping with my own money. And that made me braver than usual.

"Oooh," I said, "for a second there I was almost impressed." I whipped out my daddy's American Express Platinum Card, which he had thoughtfully provided for all my birthday shopping needs. "Now, why don't you be a nice saleslady and get me a changing room? With *alacrity*, please."

Don't get alarmed. Just because I use difficult words from time to time doesn't mean I'm a brain. I only know *alacrity*, which means "speed," because it was on one of our weekly vocabulary tests this past year and our English teacher, Mr. Blanchard, is a total babe. I kid you not. He looks like Brad Pitt, only smarter. For one whole school year I lived, slept, and breathed the dictionary, just hoping Mr. Blanchard would notice me. He didn't, but I did learn the exact definition of 1,187 new words. I try to use them from time to time, as a tribute to what could have been the love of my young life.

Meredith took one look at the plastic in my hand and stomped off toward the back of the store. "One moment, please," she said over her shoulder.

Normally I wouldn't even be shopping at a store

like Boutique Chic, but I had had my eye on this blouse ever since I saw it in the window back in May. Now it was the end of June, and I still couldn't get it out of my head. How could I? It was perfect: electric blue, sleeveless, made of hand-finished silk and lace. And I know it sounds weird, but I felt as if I'd seen it somewhere before, as if I was somehow *meant* to have it. I wanted to hold it, to touch it, to take it home with me.

That was just like me, to have a major crush on a piece of designer clothing.

As I watched Meredith walking away with her weird, high hair style and her bizarre spike-heeled shoes, I had another thought: Maybe Boutique Chic *didn't* hire Parisians. Maybe they hired aliens.

It would make a lot of sense. For one thing, it would fit right in with Metier's reputation as an intergalactic hot spot. People here are always seeing strange lights in the night sky. When two kids from my school disappeared this year, all anyone could talk about was how they had probably been abducted by extraterrestrials.

Personally, I have a hard time believing in all this UFO business. I mean, let's say that there *were* some kind of alien creatures out there and that they developed neutrino power or whatever so that they could travel into space. It would take forever to get anywhere, and they'd have to build their spaceship really small and cramped, with absolutely *no* closet space. How would they know what clothes to bring? I have trouble packing an overnight bag.

I'm rambling. But let's suppose these aliens decided to land on Earth. Would they really land in *Wisconsin?* Wouldn't they go somewhere more fashionable, like New York or Italy? Or maybe the Virgin Islands? If this supersophisticated, technologically advanced alien culture asked me, I would tell them: *Skip cow country altogether.*

I sure wish *I* could.

It *is* horrible about the missing kids, Elena Vargas and Todd Aldridge. And it's kind of scary. After all, they *were* abducted by someone, even if it wasn't by aliens. My dad like, *obsesses* every time I'm out after dark.

That's why tonight I was shopping with my two best friends—Lynette Barbini and Kara White. Lynette is head cheerleader at Metier Junior High and Kara is, if anything, even better looking. We're best buds because we have the same fashion sense, and we go to the same swim club, and we're basically three of the most popular girls at school.

I'm not sure we'd be much good if we actually had to fight off an attacker, but we could certainly teach him to accessorize and dress a little better.

"Wow," Lynette giggled, "that was pretty funny. Did you see her face when you called her a nice saleslady?"

"She deserved it," I retorted. "She called *me* a little girl."

"I don't know," Kara said, frowning. "I think you may have hurt her feelings."

Kara was the youngest of the three of us. Lynette considered it her personal responsibility to bring Kara up to speed with the teenage world.

"Kara," Lynette said, annoyed. "It's her *job* to make us happy. Besides, she works at Boutique Chic. She doesn't *have* feelings."

"It's true," I said. "I think she may be an alien."

We all laughed.

"That's such a killer shirt," Lynette said slyly. "Maybe you can wear it tonight."

She was referring to our secret plan for later that evening. As far as our parents knew, we were going to have a sleep-over party at the Barbinis' for my birthday, just the three of us. You know, play Ouija board, Truth or Dare, and so on.

But Lynette had other games in mind. Her

older brother, Tom, was a junior at Metier High. Some of his friends were having an end-of-the-year party out by the reservoir at midnight. Lynette said we should go—we might meet some cute boys, and even if we didn't, it would really tick her older brother off.

Sneaking out of Lynette's was no problem. We had done it plenty of times and her parents, both heavy sleepers, never had a clue—not even the time we accidentally knocked a garbage can down her driveway.

I couldn't wait to go. My sixth sense was tingling—I felt sure that something out of the ordinary was going to happen tonight. I had been waiting thirteen years for something interesting to happen to me, and somehow I just *knew* that tonight was the night!

Just then Meredith the Martian returned on the scene. "We have a changing room ready for you," she said through gritted teeth. "Right this way."

"Watch out for hidden cameras," Lynette said under her breath as I walked toward the back of the store.

"Yeah, she might be recording evidence of Earth life to take back to her leader," Kara chimed in.

I smiled. We were three best friends. I knew I could count on Kara and Lynette—no matter what.

Once I was safely in the changing room, I lost no time. The blouse fit perfectly. The smooth, delicate material felt good against my skin: light, airy, beautiful. It made me look at *least* fifteen.

Lynette would be *so* jealous.

I looked into the mirror to get a second opinion. Diagnosis confirmed. The blouse *was* perfect. This was going to be the best $271 that I had ever spent. Well, okay, it was going to be the best $271 that Daddy had ever spent *on* me.

And then, without warning, it happened.

As I looked at my reflection I was hit by the most powerful sensation of déjà vu I'd ever felt. All at once I felt certain I'd actually seen this exact blouse sometime in the past. What was going on? I strained to think. Had this been in fashion years ago and was just coming back now? Were they trying to sell me old clothes? Was Boutique Chic . . . *recycling?*

No, I realized with a shock, this memory was more specific. The picture in my head was of *me—wearing* the blouse! But how could that be?

The harder I concentrated, the more sharply the memory came into focus. In fact, it was almost like looking at a snapshot. I shut my eyes tightly and examined the mental image, looking for clues, running down a checklist of features.

Hair—perfect.

Nails—perfect.

Skin—perfect. Well, one pimple. But nothing anyone would notice. Or was it?

My train of thought was broken by a loud humming noise that seemed to be coming from inside the ceiling. As it grew louder the fluorescent lights overhead started flickering. Then they went out.

Blackout!

All the fears I'd been having since I heard about the first abduction, way back in August, came flooding over me. That wigged-out feeling I'd been having about tonight—about something big happening—*this* is what it must have been about. I was going to be abducted!

Then, just as suddenly, the humming stopped. The lights flashed back on.

Now, don't judge me when I tell you that I ran out of the changing room, freaked. I was legitimately scared! Fortunately I regained my composure moments before actually bursting out into the store like some asthmatic spaz. *That* would have been classic. Instead I took a deep breath and got hold of myself as the saleslady turned around.

But to my surprise, the saleslady wasn't Meredith. It was someone else—equally strange hairstyle, makeup, and shoes, but not Meredith. I was startled. "Blackout," is all I could manage to say.

"What blackout?" the woman asked, looking confused. Her name tag read *Paula*. "What were you doing in the changing rooms?" she demanded.

"Well, *duh*," I said, "changing."

"Changing into what, exactly?"

It was nice to see that at least Boutique Chic believed in consistency: Everyone who worked there was equally rude.

"The blouse I'm wearing," I replied. "Did you see where my friends went?" I added, scanning the store. Something very strange was going on here. I noticed that the wall decorations were different than they had been a few minutes before. I mean, I understood keeping up with style, but when had they had time to change them?

"No, I didn't see your friends," Paula answered, "and that certainly is *not* one of our items—just look around you."

And that is when it hit me. Because if there is

one thing I know, it's fashion. Some people are experts in mathematics, literature, or medicine. Not me. I'm gifted at *shopping*. One look at the selection of available merchandise, and I knew that something was very, very wrong.

Unless for some reason you wanted to shop back in the *eighties*.

Vintage is one thing, but this was ridiculous. There were actually denim jackets on the racks! What was going on? Was someone playing a really over-the-top practical joke? Or had I actually teleported back in time? What was this—Narnia in a mall?

I wasn't sure about the lion or the wardrobe, but the witch was standing right in front of me. "I don't know how you snuck in here, but I'm afraid you're going to have to leave the store," she was saying.

"Wait—!" I blurted. "Wait just a sec—"

"Young lady, I don't want any trouble," Paula interrupted, getting meaner. "Leave my store now."

"But—but—!" I stammered. Okay, and how composed would *you* be after going through a time warp?

"This instant," she hissed. "You're scaring the other customers."

I realized that the other people in the store were staring at me.

"I'll leave," I retorted, finally regaining my cool, "but if the other customers are scared of anything, it's your own *contumeliousness.*"

"My what?" she asked, looking perplexed.

"It's a *vocabulary* word," I said triumphantly. "Look it up."

And with that I turned and stomped out of the boutique, not sure what I'd find waiting for me.

What I found was the mall I'd known when I was a tiny kid, preserved in every detail! It was like a little homecoming. *I missed my mall!*

I rode down the escalator, feeling like I was in a dream. I hadn't realized how much I had felt the pain of losing the Famous Amos's cookies stand, the Op and Izod clothing stores, and the old A&W Root Beer restaurant until I saw them, back in full operation. A wave of nostalgia flooded over me. This was where I had spent my childhood.

Once on the lower level I wandered over to the cinema—only one theater, playing *Back to the Future II*—and watched shoppers buying tickets. *These people have never seen* Jurassic Park! I realized. *They think that* Independence Day *is just a holiday! That* Men in Black *is how you describe priests and rabbis.*

Speaking of clothing, I suddenly noticed that everyone seemed way too warmly dressed for June. At first I thought they were just staring at me because of my excellent fashion sense—as people often do—but now I realized: They were staring at me because I was in a summer-weight blouse, skirt, and sandals, and they were all in mittens, parkas, and snow boots.

I must look ridiculous, I realized.

There's nothing I hate more than being underdressed. My mood was rapidly headed south. The full effect of what had happened hit me. *It's my thirteenth birthday*, I thought sourly, *and I'm trapped in The Land Before Time.*

I was stuck in the winter of 1989! And I was supposed to be at a party that night! With boys! It was so unfair!

I was *this close* to a meltdown. I simply *had* to find a way back. I tried to think.

Maybe I should go back to Boutique Chic and use the changing room again. Maybe it would reverse directions and return me to the future. Or would it catapult me even further into the past? I could wind up in the seventies. Yummy. Chunky shoes and bell-bottoms for cheap. But, I reminded myself, the party was in 1998. I had to be careful. Then I remembered: I'd been totally banned from Boutique Chic, anyway.

I glanced down at the notepad still held in my hand. *Triumph. Conquest. Victory. No mercy.*

I would just have to sneak back inside the House of Snob Style.

I started walking toward the elevator, where a boy dressed as the Abominable Snowman was handing out sales flyers. The sight of him cheered me up a little. I might be stuck in the past, but at least I wasn't working at the mall in a lame snowman costume.

As I passed him Snowboy looked me straight in the eyes and handed me one of the slips of paper, grinning. *Sorry, Frostface,* I thought, stepping into the elevator, *that's one sale I won't be able to make.*

The elevator doors closed. I was alone. As the elevator ascended I glanced down at the flyer, barely noticing the loud, annoying humming noise that was coming from the ceiling.

Someone had written something on the back of the slip of paper, I realized with mild interest. With my luck it was Nerdy the Snowman's phone number. But before I could make out what the words said, the lights in the elevator flickered, then went out.

It's hard being a damsel in distress when there's no one around to appreciate you. And I was *totally* distressed. *Don't freak*, I reminded myself. *You've seen* Speed. *You know what to do if an elevator stops.*

Right. Get Keanu Reeves to lower himself down the elevator shaft.

I was feeling for the alarm button when the lights flashed back on. A moment later the doors opened, and I stepped out onto the second floor.

I blinked and looked around.

There were all my familiar friends: Benetton, Contempo Casuals, and of course, The Limited.

I heaved a sigh of relief.

I was back in the present. I was safe. My pager was once again on-line.

I started walking down the corridor toward Boutique Chic. I knew Lynette and Kara would be glad to see me. They were probably going out of their minds with worry.

If I'd only known what was waiting for me, I would have been running.

In the opposite direction.

Chapter 2

I hadn't gone more than two steps before a pair of security guards stepped in front of me. "That's her," one said to the other.

"You're going to have to come with us, kid," the second guard said. "They want to talk to you at booty-cue chick." It took me a second to realize that by "booty-cue chick" he meant Boutique Chic.

I knew that Kara and Lynette would be worried about me when they didn't find me in the changing room, but this was going a little far. "I'm not a kid; I'm thirteen," I patiently explained, "and I was headed that way, anyway." Honestly, sometimes the mall can be so *trying*.

"We found her," one guard said into his walkie-talkie. "We're taking her in."

When I arrived on the scene, Kara and Lynette looked like they hadn't seen me in about two thousand years. "There she is!" Kara squealed.

"Where did you go?" Lynette demanded.

"Oh, my God," I answered them, breathless with excitement, "you're *never* going to believe what just happened to me."

It was then that I noticed Meredith the Space Saleslady glaring at me. "We believe in prosecuting shoplifters," she said. "It's store policy."

"What?" I asked, shocked. "Shoplifting? What are you talking about?"

"Tell her you didn't steal the blouse, Toni," Kara begged.

"Hold on a second," I said. "You think I *stole* this blouse from the store?" I slowly realized what was going on. They had found me outside the store, wearing the blouse—and they thought I'd boosted it! I wanted to laugh. "This is so funny," I told the stern faces in front of me. "I know what you're thinking, but I didn't steal anything. I can explain everything."

Then the awful truth hit me. What could I possibly tell them? What possible explanation could I offer that wouldn't, like, land me in a mental hospital? No one was going to believe me!

"Young lady, this is a very serious situation,"

Meredith said. "Stealing an expensive designer item from our store—"

"Oh, *right*," I snapped, annoyed, "as if I *needed* to shoplift anything. Look, why don't I just pay for the blouse and we'll call it even?"

"I'm afraid it's too late for that," Meredith replied curtly. "We have to set an example. Particularly since you were using your two friends here as accomplices—"

"Accomplices!" Lynette screeched. "But we weren't accomplices! We had no idea she was going to steal anything!"

"Lynette!" I hollered. "I *didn't* steal anything."

"So explain what happened," Kara huffed.

I couldn't believe it. My friends were turning on me! "Would someone *please* get a clue?" I said, a little too loudly. "Do I *look* like a shoplifter? Do I even *dress* like a shoplifter?"

"I've got a clue for you," Meredith said. "You're under arrest."

It was then that I remembered the two uniformed security guards behind me.

"No way," I whispered as the true horror of the situation dawned on me. "My thirteenth birthday is going to be on *Cops*."

*　　*　　*

The mall's head of security turned out to be a sour-looking bald guy with tiny little wire-framed glasses and a suit jacket that looked like it had been injection-molded from a piece of blue plastic. He sighed and pressed his fingers to the bridge of his nose. "Why don't you just admit to taking the blouse and then we can all get on with our evening?" he suggested wearily.

We'd been there over an hour. I was still wearing the blue blouse, which was swiftly losing its appeal. At that moment I'd rather have been wearing a garbage bag.

"But I didn't take it!" I insisted.

"You were just . . . wearing it outside the store."

"Paula made me leave the store," I said.

"That's an obvious lie," Meredith cut in from her chair in the corner. "Paula moved to New Mexico back in February. She hasn't worked at Boutique Chic for months."

"But this was—" I started to say, *But this was nine years ago.* Then I realized how it would sound.

"But this was . . . ?" the mall security manager prompted.

"But this was an emergency," I said in a fit of inspiration. "I was going to throw up if I spent another minute in the changing room. I'm claustrophobic."

"I didn't see you leave," Meredith said.

"You never told me you were claustrophobic before," Lynette added. I could have strangled her!

One of the security guards poked his head in the door. "The girls' parents are here," he said.

"Good," the security head said. "Let's go, kids."

We exited the room single file. Kara wouldn't even look at me.

"It's not as bad as it seems," I told Lynette as soon as she was close enough.

"It's a *felony*, Toni," Lynette replied. "That seems pretty bad to me."

"Could you be any *less* supportive?" I hissed in her ear.

"Could you be any *more* of a traitor?" she hissed back.

"I can't believe you're being so *vituperative*," I said.

Lynette stared at me blankly.

"It's a *vocabulary* word," I continued. "Listen. There's a reason for everything that happened. Believe me. It's just nothing that I can explain right now."

"That's funny," she said. "That's what I'm about to tell my mother."

There they all were, waiting in the white conference room. The Barbinis, the Whites, and my dad. I could tell you they looked happy to see us, but then I would be lying.

I think if you met my father, you'd like him. He's a total cutie and really smart, too: He's a therapist with a degree in psychology from Johns Hopkins University, which is a major college on the East Coast. The only downside about my father is, he has no fashion sense. I have to pick out everything for him—he was wearing the same little sweater vest and corduroys I'd made him wear that morning.

"Where's the girl's mother?" the mall security head barked. "This is serious business. She should be here."

"Her mother is no longer living," my dad replied. "I'm her father."

"I'm sorry," the security guy said. "I didn't know."

"Can we get on with this?" asked Mr. Barbini. He was a lawyer and always seemed to be in a hurry.

"Of course," the security chief said. "As far as we know, your daughter, Mr. Barbini, and your daughter, Mr. and Mrs. White, were not involved in this crime. I apologize for having detained them so long, but I had to release them into adult custody."

"Well, that's a relief." Mr. Barbini sighed.

"And can we go now?" Mrs. White asked.

"Yes, you're free to go with your children. All except you, Mr. Douglas. I'm going to need to talk to you about your daughter."

"Good," Mrs. Barbini said. "Our whole family has been very upset by this whole affair. Lynette, let's go."

"But we've got a slumber party tonight!" I cried.

"No," said Mrs. Barbini. "Lynette and Kara have a slumber party tonight. You're not setting foot in my house."

"Joan, please," my dad protested, "isn't that a little harsh?"

"I'm sorry, Joe," she shot back. "I like you, and Anita was a wonderful woman. But you need to take more care raising that child of yours into a lady. A *real* lady."

"But Lynette and Toni have been friends for years. Surely you're not going to separate them over something like this!"

"Yes, we are, Joe," her husband said. "I'm sorry, too, but we are. This isn't the only incident. A few weeks ago I heard someone knock over the garbage cans under my window. The next morning Lynette admitted that Toni convinced her to sneak out of the house and meet some boys by the reservoir. I hate to be the one to say this, but . . . Toni's a bad influence," Mr. Barbini concluded.

I had convinced *her!* She practically *dragged* me along! And did someone actually call *me* a bad influence on *Lynette Barbini?* Lynette, who French-kissed Trent Muldoon in *fifth grade?* My ears burned with shame.

Moments later I was alone with my dad and the Man in the Plastic Suit in the interrogation room. Kara and Lynette's parents had whisked them away, taking with them any hopes I had for a reasonably sane thirteenth birthday party.

"So what happens now?" my dad asked the security man. "Is the store going to press charges? Should I be talking to a lawyer?"

"We're not going to press charges," the security head replied. "We could, but Metier is a very small community, and we don't like to involve the police unless we have to." He smiled at my father. "No, we have a more effective way of dealing with little problems like this."

"I think this is unconstitutional," I said, my voice a hoarse whisper. "I think this is a violation of my basic rights as a human being."

I was finally back in the clothes I'd worn to the mall. All I could do was stare in horror as the security officer pushed the thumbtack into the Polaroid, sealing my doom for all time.

I don't know if it's possible to die of embarrassment, but I'm definitely about to find out.

The words above the information kiosk at the entrance to the mall read *Wall of Shame*. And there, pinned right below the *a* in *shame*, was a picture of me, looking mortified in a beautiful blue blouse. *My* photograph! For the whole world to see! The other pictures were some of the evilest and ugliest-looking faces you've ever seen. Honestly, my face was the only one up there without multiple piercings and a tattoo. I might as well have joined a gang.

I could just see my yearbook entry now: *Cheerleading (6–8), Poetry Club (7, 8), Stole Things from the Mall (8).*

"Can we leave now?" my dad asked the security head.

"You're free to go," he said. "But young lady, I'd watch your step from now on."

Maybe that was what had happened to the boy handing out flyers in that snowman suit—maybe it was his sentence for some unspeakable crime, like dipping his feet in the mall fountain or accidentally going into the girls' room. Who would have thought that my favorite mall favored cruel and unusual punishment?

The walk through the parking lot was the longest of my entire life. The skies were black and cloudy—just like my mood. About thirty feet from the car thunder boomed and it started to pour. By the time we got the doors open and slid into the front seat, I looked like a drowned hamster.

Well, I thought, shivering, *at least I can officially say that this is the worst thirteenth birthday in history.*

"Daddy," I said as he started the car, "I didn't steal that blouse."

"It's okay, sugar," he replied. "You don't have to say anything. It's my fault. I haven't been enough of a father to you."

"No, Daddy," I said. "I mean I *really* didn't steal that blouse! Honest!"

My father reached over and took my hand in his.

"Sweetheart, whatever happened, I'm sure there was a good reason for it. From now on, we're going to spend more time together." He gave my hand a squeeze.

"You're not listening to me," I said. "I'm trying to tell you that I didn't shoplift. I know it seems like I did, but something else was going on."

"I believe you," he said. Then we drove for a while in an uncomfortable, tense silence. Finally he said, "If you'd like to tell me what really happened, you can. I'll just sit here and listen."

I ran my fingers through my damp hair and bit my lip. I always told Daddy everything—well, almost everything. In a lot of ways he was my best friend. But if I told him this, wouldn't he think I was mental?

"Daddy," I said carefully, "what I'm about to tell you—can you promise just to listen to me, without making any judgments about me, for a few seconds?"

"Sure, sugar," he said, looking more concerned than I'd ever seen him. Great. Now I'd really done it.

I had no choice but to continue. "The truth about what happened is . . ." I swallowed hard. Here was the moment of truth. "The truth is, I went back in time."

He nodded. "I'm not judging. Continue."

"I stepped into the changing room and the lights flickered and there was this weird noise, and when I stepped out—well, ran out, actually, because I was pretty nervous, but anyway—when I came out,

27

everything had changed. It was *1989*, Daddy. And the saleslady there was surprised and made me leave the store. Then when I came back to the present, they thought I'd left without paying."

That was convincing. Even I didn't believe me, and I had been there.

"You say you went back to 1989? Nine years ago?"

Could it be? Did he believe me after all? "Yes, Daddy, and there was a Famous Amos cookie stand, the exact one we used to go to, and—"

"Hold on a second," he said, never taking his eyes off the road. It was really starting to pour out. The air had that swampy, mossy smell that you get in a summertime rain. "Let's just slow down for a moment and consider what we know."

My hopes fell. "You don't believe me!" I accused him. "You think I'm lying."

"Whoa. Did I say you were lying? I think you're telling me the truth. But sometimes things seem real to us that aren't real. Sometimes our mind plays tricks on us. Our imagination takes over."

My dad was using his Doctor Voice. The same voice I'd heard him use on the phone with his patients. "Great," I muttered. "Nobody understands me. Not you, not my former best friends. Nobody at all."

"Well," he replied, "I was getting to that. We're very close, Toni, and I love you more than anything, but in a way you're right. I don't understand you completely. I was never a twelve-year-old girl, for one thing. When you said 1989, it made me think. Nine years ago is when we lost your mother. Today is your thirteenth birthday. What could be more natural than wanting to see your mom on this, the most important day in your career as a kid?"

"So," I said slowly, "you think that I wanted to see her so badly that I somehow traveled backward in time?"

"Not exactly," he replied, "but I do think you wanted to see her badly enough to *believe* you were back at a time when she was still alive."

"You still don't understand," I muttered, trying not to cry. I turned away from him and looked at the fat raindrops splashing against the window.

"Maybe I don't, Toni," he said softly. "Maybe I don't understand. But if you did go back, I think you're lucky. Sometimes I try to go back there myself . . . but I never make it."

Suddenly I felt an enormous flood of sympathy for my father wash over me. He had loved Mom so much. And he missed her every day of his life.

I put a hand on his shoulder. He leaned over and kissed the top of my head.

I glanced in the backseat. There was a pink bakery box sitting next to a wrapped present. "Is that a birthday cake back there?" I asked.

"Yes," he replied. "I kind of guessed how the Barbinis would react when the mall called me. I thought you might need some cheering up."

Didn't I say my daddy was the best?

"Thanks, Daddy," I said, sniffling a little from the cold. "Consider me cheered."

The car bounced over the wooded country road leading back to our part of town. Rain beat steadily on the top and windows. The fog was becoming so thick that it was hard to see more than fifteen feet ahead of us.

And that's when the death occurred.

Chapter 3

Dad slammed the hood of the car. "Well," he announced, "the car's dead, all right."

Hey, I never said it was a *human* death.

"I don't know what the heck could be the matter," he continued, scooting back into the driver's seat. "It's like someone sucked all the electricity out of the car. It's not the alternator, there's nothing leaking. . . ."

We had been driving along, just like I said, when suddenly the radio shut off, the lights went out, and the engine died. It was as though someone had flipped a big off switch.

"Maybe it was the lightning," I suggested.

"Maybe it was . . . aliens," he teased.

"Maybe it was your bad jokes," I shot back.

"Maybe it was that security guy from the mall," Dad said. "Our poor car was so upset by the way he treated you that it decided life wasn't worth living anymore."

I giggled. "What are we going to do now?" I asked.

"Well," he said, "there's a gas station not too far from here. I'm gonna hoof it. You're going to stay with the car. Don't want you getting eaten up by wolves on your thirteenth birthday."

Now that he mentioned it, it was kind of spooky out. There was no moon—it was pitch-dark—and we were in the middle of nowhere. I know that by the time you're my age, you're not supposed to be afraid of walking outside in the dark, but, well . . . "If you insist," I replied.

Daddy reached over, grabbed an umbrella from the glove compartment, and headed out into the storm. I sat in the car, watching him walk away. He grew smaller and smaller until, suddenly, he was swallowed up by the rain and inky blackness. I was alone.

Rain rapped and drummed on the surface of our little Volvo. The fog had really rolled in, covering the ground in a thick cottony shroud. Without the windshield wipers the view through the front window was like looking at a wet blackboard.

It was *mondo* creepy.

Generally, once I make up my mind, I don't change it for anything. But I was beginning to reconsider my decision to stay with the car.

To take my mind off the situation, I started to go over the day's events. What had really happened back in the mall? Maybe Daddy was right. Maybe my brain *was* playing tricks on me. I could have run out of the store when Kara and Lynette weren't looking, I supposed. And then I could have hallucinated the rest.

But it had seemed so real! Was I losing my mind? Isn't that the definition of insanity—when you can't tell the difference between fantasy and reality?

Am I going crazy?

I shifted uncomfortably in my seat and tried not to think about it. I was still wearing my seat belt. Reaching to unfasten it, I felt something poking out of my skirt pocket. It was the flyer that Snowboy had given me.

Wait a second. The flyer! If I had it . . . it meant I really *had* traveled back in time. It was proof!

I eagerly unfolded it, holding it up to the window. I had to peer closely at it to make anything out in the gloom.

Unfortunately it was just a mint green square of paper with information about a Christmas sale. There was no date, no mention of the year, nothing that would support my story. It wasn't proof at all.

Then I remembered the writing on the back. I flipped it over. As if on cue, a brilliant lightning bolt flashed across the sky, illuminating the note. A strangely familiar handwriting came into sharp focus:

NO, YOU 'RE NOT CRAZY,
BUT YOU ARE IN DANGER.
TAKE THE CAKE OUT. NOW.

Is there anything crazier than finding a note that says "you're not crazy"? And what did *that* mean, "take the cake out"? That was the craziest thing of all!

I was too weak with shock to argue—particularly with a note. I might as well see what it meant. As thunder boomed overhead I reached into the backseat and carefully picked up the ominous pink bakery box.

Was the cake the dangerous thing? I wondered. It didn't feel heavy enough to be a bomb. Unless it was a really *light* bomb. I ask you, do I seem like a girl who deserves to be blown up by her own birthday cake? I still had prom ahead of me, and that wasn't for four years!

Ever so carefully I lifted the top off the box, fully expecting to see wires and a ticking clock or at the very least a frightening message spelled out in lethal green frosting, like something out of Alice in Wonderland. The cake read:

HAPPY 13TH BIRTHDAY, TONI

That was it? *That* was the danger? I felt like laughing at myself for getting so worked up. I had just been frightened by a cake.

Girl, you have got to get a grip.

Just then the lightning flashed again, revealing several figures approaching the car. My dad, with help. I heaved a sigh of relief. He'd probably find the whole cake incident funny to the extreme.

As he stepped up to the car I unlocked the door and rolled down the window. "Hello," I was about to say, "did you miss me?"

But then I saw his face.

You know how your brain works in slow motion in a panic situation? Mine went into deep freeze. The first thought I had was, *That's not my daddy.* Then I thought, *He looks familiar, but where have I seen him before?* Then I thought, *Oh, yeah, I saw him at the mall.*

Or rather, I saw his picture.

Next to *my* picture.

In the gallery of known criminals.

Oh. My. God.

It was the gang of punk teenagers that had their pictures tacked up next to mine!

With a little yelp I managed to get the car window rolled up before he could stick his hand inside. Thank goodness for child safety locks! They had been put on the car when I was little to stop me from crawling out—now they were stopping these creeps from getting in. I quickly slapped down the locks all around the automobile.

The scene that followed was like something out of a horror movie! Pale skin, pierced noses, hair dyed all different colors—I guess looking cool for these guys meant the same as looking like circus clowns from hell. There were four of them, circling the car, slapping at the windows with their ripped leather gloves.

"Hey, little girl," the leader sneered, a skinny guy with crazy cherry red hair, "come out and play with us!"

"Yeah, play with us!" repeated the biggest of

the four, a really fat, stupid-looking guy with a tattoo on his forehead and a thick black mohawk.

Winner, I thought as his ugly face leered up against the window glass.

"Don't you guys have better things to do?" I suggested helpfully. "Don't you have to go smoke cigarettes or do drugs or something?"

One of the punks started jumping on the trunk. Another gang member methodically kicked in the car's headlights, taillights, and parking lights, one bulb at a time.

"Why don't you get out of the car," the skinny gang leader said, grinning evilly, "so that we don't have to come in there after you?"

"Why don't you go pierce each other?" I shot back.

That was when they started rocking the car. Fortunately Volvos are very solidly built cars, which is why Mom insisted we buy one. But I was beginning to get majorly seasick. "You'll never get inside," I explained. "The Volvo S70 is the sturdiest automobile in its class."

Just then the driver's side window came crashing in with a shower of glass. Oops. I guess the owner's warranty doesn't cover getting smashed with a rock.

"I'm sorry," said the fat boy, leaning through

the gaping hole where the window had been, "did I hurt your little car?"

I decided it was time to use the cake.

Without thinking, I whipped it out of the box and slammed it as hard as I could into the guy's face. Sponge cake, frosting, and sprinkles went flying everywhere.

"I'm sorry," I shouted at him. "Did I hurt your little face?"

"You little—!" he shouted, trying to wipe the gooey chocolate frosting out of his eyes. "I'm going to mess you up!"

"If you can catch me," I said. In one swift motion I unlocked the door, pulled on the handle, and kicked the door open with both feet. It caught the fat boy right in the stomach. He exhaled hard and fell over backward into the mud.

I leaped out of the car. Fortunately the other three members of the gang were on the other side. I took off into the woods as fast as my legs would take me.

All those years of cheerleading practice were paying off as I flew over the gravel and mud, dashing through the dark, storm-swept woods. It was sheer luck that kept me from running headfirst into a tree trunk. I kept my arms up in front of me as I ran, swiping back branches before they could slap me in the face. Even so, other, lower branches tore at my clothes while unseen foliage scratched at my legs and arms like tiny claws.

Still, it was preferable to being back in the car.

I had never seen so much lightning. The jagged streaks of electricity crackled through the night sky and thunder roared all around, as if Metier was under attack by an enemy army. I glanced over my shoulder as a thunderbolt bathed the woods in blinding blue-white light.

The punks were right behind me!

As fast as I was, the high schoolers were faster—and they were *mad*.

Just when I thought all was lost, I saw it. The sign of a service station, shining at the top of a steep hill. That must be the one that Daddy was talking about. The giant yellow shell was like a blazing beacon against the foggy night. I was saved!

The gang members were too close to waste any time. I couldn't take the gradual, grassy path up the side of the hill. I ran directly up the steep embankment, scrabbling at the dirt and gravel with my hands, digging the toes of my sandals into the muddy ground. My breath came in pitiful little gasps. I was almost there. I was so close.

Then all at once the ground underneath me gave way. I was falling! I tumbled, sliding and spinning, down the embankment, my head and elbows bouncing against the sharp rocks. I landed in a big, muddy, scum-covered puddle. The gang members were around me in no time . . . and they didn't look happy.

"Get her up," the fat one said. He was still covered in mud and frosting. He was clutching his stomach where the car door had hit him. "I want her to get a good look at me."

Two of the others stepped forward. They grabbed my arms, pulling me to my feet.

"You think you're pretty smart, don't you, little girl?" the gang leader asked in his high, scratchy voice.

"No," I said honestly. "I think I'm cold, miserable, and hungry. I think I'm having the worst birthday in recorded history. I think I'm getting a cold." I realized I was having a meltdown, but I was too far gone to care. "Do you want to know what else I think? I think this whole evening has been unfair! I think I deserve to be somewhere warm and dry! I think I deserve presents! I think I deserve to be at a party, and happy, and not accused of shoplifting, and not betrayed by my friends, and not stuck out in the middle of nowhere surrounded by a bunch of . . . *troglodytes* like you!"

They looked at me blankly.

"It's a *vocabulary* word," I screamed, "look it up!"

The leader of the gang walked around me, looking me over. I gulped. Having attitude was one thing, but this time I'd gone too far, and I knew it.

"I don't know about any troglomites or whatever you're talking about," the leader said. "But I'll *tell you* what you deserve. You deserve to be taught a lesson for what you did to my man Pluto, here." He patted the fat boy with the mohawk on the back.

"Your name is Pluto?" I asked. "Sorry."

"Okay," the fat boy shouted, furious, "that's it!"

He pulled something out of his black leather jacket. It was about eight inches long and metal. He pressed a button, and a metal blade flicked out.

It was a switchblade. I was being held at knifepoint.

Why was this turning out to be the worst birthday *ever*? Why wasn't I somewhere being adored by really cute boys? Why was this happening to *me*?

"I don't care if you *are* a girl," he said, "and I don't care if you're only a little kid. Nobody makes fun of my name."

He took a step closer. I held my breath, waiting for the inevitable. And that's when it happened.

I sneezed.

I know, it wasn't the best time for a sneeze. But I was cold, and damp, and I'm allergic to mold and spores.

Suddenly the night was electrified by a brilliant pink-white light. Electricity crackled along the surface of the mud puddle, rising up the legs of my assailants!

The last thing I remembered was the entire gang being wrapped up in bands of electricity that coiled around them like fiery snakes. The four punks howled and screamed as the dancing threads of power jumped from earring to nose ring to lip stud.

Daddy always warned me that multiple piercings weren't safe, I thought idly as I watched the light show; *now I know why*.

Then I passed out. There's only so much a "little kid" can take.

Chapter 4

I woke up surrounded by what looked like the entire cast of *ER*. I was in a hospital. That made sense. I wondered if I had been hurt badly. My heart froze: Was I going to be scarred? I had seen a movie of the week about a beautiful model who had been in a car wreck and had to go through, like, years of reconstructive surgery just to look human again. Was that the fate that awaited me?

Daddy was standing by my bedside, looking adorably worried. Next to him was a man who looked vaguely familiar, but I couldn't quite place him. Where had I seen him before? Oh, that's right, he was weird Ethan Rogers's dad. He had come in for career day. What did he do for a living again?

That was when I saw what he was wearing: a steel gray police uniform with a gold star over the breast pocket. Finally I remembered: Ethan's dad was the chief of police! And behind him was another officer, a tall, cute younger guy whose name tag read *Whaley*. What were the police doing at my hospital bed?

Would the horror of this birthday never end?

"I didn't steal the blouse!" I practically shouted. "I never shoplifted anything in my entire life! Except for a teensy candy bracelet, and that was in second grade!"

"What blouse?" Officer Whaley asked.

"No one's here about a shoplifting," Chief Rogers said.

"Take it easy, sugar," my dad said, stroking my cheek. "Just relax. Lie back now."

"What's she talking about?" Officer Whaley whispered to my father.

"Dwayne, why don't you hold the questions for a minute?" Chief Rogers said. Then he turned to me. "Toni, we're here because you were attacked tonight. Do you remember that?"

It was slowly coming back to me. Being trapped in the car . . . the nightmarish run through the woods . . . the electricity crackling over the surface of the water. "Yes," I said. "I remember everything. *Am I going to be scarred?*"

"No, angel, you're fine," Daddy replied. "You're not hurt at all."

"I feel exhausted," I said, sinking down in my pillow. It was true. I barely had the strength to open my eyes.

"I'm sorry to be asking you these questions now," Chief Rogers said, "especially because I know what a terrible ordeal you've been through. But it's important that I get the details while they're still fresh in your mind. Do you know who I am?"

"You're Ethan's dad, right?" I replied.

"That's right," he said, "and I'm also the chief of police for Metier Township. Right now we have four teens in custody in connection with your attack. They're real troublemakers. We've charged them with vandalism and assault with a deadly weapon, but we're going to need your help to make it stick. Do you think you could pick them out of a lineup if you had to?"

"Pick them out of a lineup?" I laughed weakly. "I can get you their photographs."

"What do you mean?" the chief asked.

"They're hanging up in the mall," I answered.

"On that bulletin board of shoplifters, next to mine."

"You're a shoplifter?" Officer Whaley asked, startled.

"It's a long story," Daddy interjected.

"Let's start with the actual assault," Chief Rogers said, giving Officer Whaley a sharp look. "Can you tell me how it happened?"

"I was in the car," I said, "waiting for my father to get back from the service station. Four guys came up out of nowhere. I guess we just broke down in the wrong place at the wrong time. Suddenly they were all over the car, banging on the windows, jumping up and down on the trunk—and then one of them broke a window with a rock."

"Can you tell me which one did the actual damage?"

"I think his name is Pluto," I answered.

"Did you do anything at any time to provoke him?"

"I told him I was sorry about his name," I replied.

"Told him she was sorry about his name," Officer Whaley muttered to himself, scribbling in a little black police book.

"Dwayne," Chief Rogers sighed, "why don't you wait in the hall for a few minutes. Toni, what happened next? How did you react?"

"I managed to get out of the car," I answered, "and then I ran as fast as I could. I tried to run up the hill to the service station, but I slipped and fell back down it. That's when they got me."

"How did you fight them off?"

"I didn't really," I said, frowning as I remembered the scene. "They were about to hurt me, and then suddenly they got hit by the lightning."

"Lightning, huh?" Chief Rogers said.

"I'm sorry, but that's impossible," said a gray-haired woman in a white doctor's coat. I realized she'd been there the whole time, standing next to the foot of the bed and quietly listening. "My name is Dr. Strickrichter, Toni. Those boys weren't hit by lightning."

"But Doctor," the chief said, "they clearly suffered a tremendous electric shock."

"I agree," she said, "but it wasn't from lightning. If it was lightning, there would have been scorch marks on their shoes and clothing and burns on their skin. But their injuries were minor, and their clothing was untouched."

"But I saw it," I insisted. "There was a sudden

flash of pink-white light, and then this burst of electricity hit them."

"Could it have been some alternate form of lightning?" Daddy asked. "Ball lightning or something?"

"We don't know if ball lightning even exists," Dr. Strickrichter answered. "But even if it does, this wasn't it. No, this was a low-amperage, high-voltage source of energy. If I had to guess, I'd say it came from a stun gun."

A stun gun! "Could somebody else have . . . ambushed them? Someone lurking in the woods?" my father asked.

"It's unlikely," Chief Rogers replied. "In that re-mote place, after dark, in the middle of a storm—and let's not forget, she was deep in the woods—it's hard to believe some guy would be waiting out there with a taser. Still, that's the only theory we have to work with. It'll have to do for now."

What was going on? There wasn't anybody else in the woods with us—now that I thought about it, I was sure of it. If it wasn't lightning, what had electrified those punks? And why hadn't I been hurt, too?

I was struck with a crazy thought.

Had *I* done it somehow?

"*You* didn't have a stun gun on you, did you, Toni?" Officer Whaley asked from the doorway, and the whole room laughed.

"Ha, ha," I laughed, fluttering my eyelashes, trying my best to look like a little angel—preferably one that didn't pack a weapon.

"They're transferring the suspects to the state hospital," Dr. Strickrichter said. "They're loading them now, but they haven't left yet. You can still catch them if you hurry."

"What do you say, Toni?" Chief Rogers asked. "Do you feel up to making an ID?"

The truth was, I didn't. I felt like the ground was crumbling from underneath me and I was sliding, sliding, sliding down a hill, losing all hope of sanity and ruining a perfectly good pair of shoes in the process.

At times such as this one, you have to go back to the basics. You have to dig deep inside yourself and ask, What is the right thing to do? What would my idols do? What would Posh Spice do?

"I'll do it," I said.

When we arrived in the hospital loading bay, we had no trouble finding the four gang members: All we had to do was follow our ears.

"I'm not going!" shouted a high, scratchy voice. I recognized it as belonging to the red-headed leader. "Get your hands off me!"

"You wouldn't be such a big man without that gun and badge," I heard Pluto shouting at the same time. "Give me a fair fight, and I'll pulp you good."

We came around a row of parked ambulances—Daddy, Chief Rogers, Officer Whaley, and myself—to see two more police officers struggling with the four teens. The punks were refusing to get into the police van that would take them to the maximum-security state hospital. The officers were red in the face from trying to make them go by force—the gang members were pretty strong, and it was four against two.

The first thing I noticed about the gang members was that they were handcuffed to one another. The second thing I noticed was their hair: It stood straight up off their heads, like Troll dolls'! I guess the electricity that hit them left them in a permanent state of static cling.

"Nice haircuts," I said when we got within earshot. "Who's your stylist—Dennis Rodman?"

The gang leader slowly turned around, a look of horror on his face. When he saw me, his jaw dropped open with a silent scream.

Fortunately Pluto was there to fill in the gap. "*Aiiiyeee!*" he screamed. "It's *her!*" He desperately scrambled into the back of the police van, dragging the other gang members along behind him.

"Keep her away from us!" the red-haired gang leader rasped, cowering behind one of the officers. "She'll hurt us! You gotta take us to jail *now!*"

"Please!" Pluto shrieked. "Before she comes closer!"

Chief Rogers, Officer Whaley, and Daddy stood watching the scene in shocked silence, unable to believe what they were seeing. Then they looked down at me.

"Yeah," I said finally. "That's definitely them."

Chapter 5

As Doctor Strickrichter signed my release papers Daddy turned to me and said, "There's a surprise waiting for you back at the ranch."

I groaned.

"A good surprise," Daddy said quickly. "A surprise that you'll like."

"Okay," I said reluctantly. "But it better not involve Rochelle."

"Weeeell," he said. "What if it involves Rochelle a little?"

"Daddy!"

Rochelle was Daddy's girlfriend and had been for three years. I'm not exactly sure where the name *Rochelle* comes from, but I think it's Greek for "she who sticks her nose in where it doesn't belong." I was beginning to suspect that she and Daddy were going to get married. To be honest, I think they would have gotten married a long time ago—if I hadn't stood in their way.

I suppose I could see why Daddy liked her. Even I had to admit that she was beautiful. She had long, honey brown hair that she wore in an elegant knot; slender, delicately tapered fingers with perfectly done nails; and enormous, bright hazel eyes that widened or narrowed depending on whether she was interested in what you had to say or interested in telling you a secret. I was a little jealous of her figure. I couldn't wait until my body started to look like that!

And that wasn't all. Four days a week, Rochelle volunteered as a nurse at an old folks' home in town called Falling Pines—which, call me crazy, doesn't sound like the safest place for a bunch of people in wheelchairs. The rest of the week she taught classes at the Metier Junior College extension school, classes with titles like "How to Make Your Enemies Your Friends" and "Everyone Needs a Hug Sometime." Puke city.

I guess the thing about Rochelle really is, she's not Mom. And no matter how hard she tries to be perfect, it just points up the fact that she isn't. She keeps trying to do the right thing, but she always winds up making things worse. I think she'd be a lot happier if she just forgot about Daddy and moved on to someone else. I know *I* would be.

"I phoned Ro from the service station to tell her we'd be late," Daddy said. "Then, when she heard what had happened, she was very worried about you."

"Why is she always worried about me?" I cried. "Can't she worry about someone else's daughter for a change?"

"She's just trying to show an interest in your life, Toni," he replied. "She feels like she's part of the family."

"Well, she *isn't* part of the family, and if she *feels* like changing her last name to Douglas," I said, "I hope you remind her that she's not married to you yet." Okaaay. Sorry, folks—that was the dark side of my personality making an appearance. "Daddy, just, please—not tonight? Please? Can we call her and cancel?"

"Too late," he whispered.

I turned around and followed the direction he was looking. There in the doorway stood Rochelle, wearing a dress that was more appropriate for the Academy Awards than for a hospital ward at midnight.

"*There* she is!" she exclaimed, holding out her arms to me. "How's my favorite newest thirteen-year-old?"

"Nauseated," I replied, staring directly at her. I gave her my best fake smile.

"Toni . . . ," Daddy warned under his breath.

"Nauseated from the medicine they gave me for the, uh, concussion," I continued, covering gracefully.

"Is she going to be all right, Joe?" Rochelle asked, concerned.

"Aside from a major case of smarty-pants, she'll be fine," Daddy replied. "Let's get home. I heard a rumor about a replacement cake that's probably melting as we speak."

I suppressed another groan. The longest night of my life was about to get even longer.

We had to take Rochelle's car on the ride home since our poor Volvo had been towed to the body shop. As she drove I told her all about the evening's events. She was suitably impressed.

"And he actually had a knife?" she asked, her eyes growing wide in the rearview mirror.

"A switchblade," I replied proudly.

"Okay, that's enough reliving that gang attack for one night," Daddy said from the passenger seat. I think he was still feeling guilty about having left me by myself.

"You know, I was thinking," Rochelle said.

Don't strain yourself, I felt like adding.

"Now that you're thirteen," Rochelle went on, "we have to start giving some serious thought to your name."

"What do you mean?" I asked.

"Just that your name, Antonia, is so beautiful," she replied. "Now that you're a lady, maybe you'd like to try going by your full name or even just Ann. You don't want to be Toni all your life— people will think you're a boy!"

"My mother said I'd always be her little Toni," I told her abruptly. "She never called me Antonia unless I'd broken something."

We drove on in stony silence for a few minutes.

"Well, there I go again, putting my foot in my mouth," Rochelle said.

"It's fine," I replied.

"I'm sorry, Toni, I was just trying to say something nice," she continued.

"Really, it's fine," I told her.

"I feel *so* stupid," she said.

Not as stupid as you look, I said to myself as we pulled into the driveway.

"So, how many for cake?" Daddy asked, with that look on his face that he gets when he's trying to avert a major disaster.

"A stereo!" I exclaimed, looking at the box in the center of the wrapping paper strewn all over the floor. "Daddy, I can't believe it!"

"It's got a five-CD changer," he told me. "So I guess now you can play that annoying music five times as much."

"It's not annoying," I clarified, "it's *upbeat.*"

"You'd think by now I'd have learned the difference," he said.

"Mine next," Rochelle said, handing me a wrapped gift box. "Happy birthday, sweetheart."

I suppose it was nice of Rochelle to buy me something for my birthday. I'd never gotten her anything for hers—although now that I thought about it, I didn't remember her ever celebrating one. I guess if *I* were almost forty, I wouldn't want to remind people that I was getting older, either.

I ripped the paper off the box. *Boutique Chic*, the glossy gold lettering read. Uh-oh.

I opened the package. My face fell.

"I saw you drooling over it in the window last week," Rochelle said happily.

It was the blouse. The blouse that had started all my problems.

Didn't I say Rochelle had a talent for doing exactly the wrong thing?

"You shouldn't have spent so much money," Daddy said. We were both staring, ashen faced, at the electric blue shirt.

"Don't you want to try it on, sweetheart?" Rochelle asked.

"Maybe later," I managed to choke out. "I'm a little tired."

"Do you know what I heard?" she asked. "Some crazy girl tried to steal this very blouse earlier tonight! In fact—"

"You know, Ro," Daddy interrupted, seeing that dangerous look on my face that announced I was about to go nuclear, "I think Toni had maybe just better go on to bed. She's been through a lot today, and it's way past her bedtime."

"Oh, well, I understand," Rochelle said. "Okay, sweetheart, I know it doesn't make up for everything that's happened to you, but wear it in good health."

"Thanks," I said. "I will."

Or at least I'd try to.

* * *

I awoke the next morning to the second-worst sensation in the world. The worst sensation is, of course, asking your stylist for "just a trim" and then discovering that he's gone Apache on your scalp. The second worst is waking up to a blaring alarm clock—when you've barely slept at all.

I reached over and glared at the clock. The digital display read twelve-fifteen. Thank heaven for summer vacations. I reached out to turn off the terrible noise, but the minute my fingers brushed the surface of the clock, a strange thing happened. It went dead. Completely dead. Not only did the alarm stop buzzing, but the red numbers winked out.

"That's funny," I said out loud, but inside I didn't find it funny at all. Yesterday the car had gone mysteriously dead and now this. What next? I made a mental note to stay away from anyone with a pacemaker.

I lifted the clock off the nightstand and was instantly filled with a weird, dizzy, tingling sensation. It seemed to flow out of the clock and up my arm and settle in my stomach.

Suddenly I knew what it was like to be a carbonated soda. I felt refreshed, alert, tingling . . . *effervescent*.

I leaped out of bed, ready to start the day.

Maybe this was just what being thirteen was like: Every day would feel great. And I had the whole summer ahead of me.

Daddy must have brought my presents into my room while I was asleep. My new stereo was sitting on my dresser, next to the blouse from Boutique Chic.

Twelve-fifteen in the afternoon. The perfect time to try out the new No Doubt CD.

I lifted the stereo out of its box and placed it on my desk. I read the instructions carefully. Well, okay, I didn't read the instructions at all. But who does? I don't even understand why they make them. If you plug it in and it works, great. If not, they should find a way to make it easier to use.

Plug it in. Right. There was an outlet underneath my desk, but it was kind of hard to get to. I pulled back the desk chair, then got down on my hands and knees. Crawling under the desk, I wedged my hand into the narrow space between the desk and the wall. But when I tried gliding the plug into the socket, it wouldn't fit.

I withdrew my hand and examined the plug. One of the prongs looked bent. Great. It looked like I'd need something to straighten the prong out. I figured I might as well try using my fingers before going downstairs to get Daddy's pliers.

The minute I touched the prong, there was a sudden, loud, and terrifying noise from directly above me! I tried to stand up, forgetting that I was underneath the desk, and walloped my head on the hard bottom surface. I dropped the plug and the noise stopped as suddenly as it started.

I didn't realize what had just happened until I figured out what the sound was. It was the opening chords of the new Backstreet Boys single—which must have been playing on the radio. But how had the stereo turned on all by itself?

Rubbing my head, I crawled out from under the desk and faced the silent stereo. It just sat there. Innocently. As if it hadn't just violated all known laws of major appliances. I glared at it.

But by now I had an inkling of what was going on. I gathered up the cord slowly, never letting the stereo out of my sight. Then, with a feeling of great trepidation, I touched the prongs again.

Instantly the stereo lit up; the music blared. It wasn't loud, I remembered. It was *upbeat*.

Somehow I was making the stereo turn on.

I had proof. I wasn't going crazy after all! I had to show Daddy!

I leaped to my feet and was about to run over to

my father's bedroom when my eyes fell on the mysterious blue blouse. For some odd reason I felt oddly compelled to try it on again. I hadn't even showered yet, I told myself. But I was drawn to it. It was as if it was calling to me. Like it was daring me to put it on. I knew it was what I had to do. I knew, somehow, that it was the next step in my destiny.

Well, for some of us, trying on clothes is very important.

Moments later I stood in front of the full-length mirror on my closet door, trying to figure out why I was dressed for a party at twelve-thirty in the afternoon. Then as I watched myself I was reminded of the image I'd had in the changing room of Boutique Chic. I smoothed down my hair and put it back in a ribbon. I put on the same pair of shoes, the same skirt, the same anklet and bracelet I'd seen in my mind's eye.

Then I grabbed my mini-backpack. I wasn't sure how I knew, but I could tell I was going somewhere.

The same creepy sense of déjà vu came over me. I now looked exactly like I did in the vision! It was too eerie for words, like that moment in a horror movie when the background music stops and you just know some psycho is about to jump out with a knife.

63

The lights flickered. A loud humming noise grew steadily overhead. Then it faded.

I heard someone approaching in the hall. "Dad?" I called out. I took a step toward my door, pulling it open. "Did you just hear that—"

The words caught in my throat.

Because it wasn't my father at all.

Chapter 6

It was someone I hadn't seen in a very long time. She wore a housedress with little purple flowers on it and earrings to match. I knew that dress. I had pulled on its hem so many times before, following it around shopping centers, looking up to see that warm, comforting face at the top.

"Mom!" I cried, stepping toward her.

My mother raised her finger to her lips, signaling me to be quiet. She entered my room and closed the door softly behind her.

I couldn't believe it. Here I was with my mother again, the one person I never expected to see for the rest of my life. Now I could reach out and touch her.

For the first time I noticed how different my

room looked. The tiger-stripe bedspread I bought last summer had been switched with a Little Mermaid one. There were rainbow curtains on the windows—the same ones Daddy had replaced with miniblinds years ago. My posters of Will Smith, No Doubt, and the Spice Girls were gone; in their places were finger paintings and crayon drawings. I recognized a turkey hand cutout marked Thanksgiving, 1989, from the Wee Care nursery school. I reeled from the shock. My room was just like it had been nine years ago.

And so was my mother.

She looked just like I remembered her but different at the same time. One thing I'd forgotten was how beautiful she looked in the simplest of outfits. She had an inner beauty that shone right through. Maybe if I stopped covering my own face over with gunk from Cover Girl, I'd see it in me, too.

I threw my arms around my mother and hugged her like I'd never let her go.

"There, there," she murmured. "There, there. Everything's okay, my little Toni."

When I heard her call me that, I burst out crying. How could she understand how much I had missed her? How could everything be "okay" when nothing in my life was making sense?

When I finally let go, I blurted out the question I had wanted to ask since the whole crazy thing had started. "What's happening to me?" I asked. "How did I get here?"

"I programmed you to come to me," my mother said. "That's how you got here."

"What do you mean, programmed?" I snuffled, still trying to control my tears. "Like a VCR?"

My mother laughed delicately. "Kind of. You know how your VCR has a little computer chip inside it that tells it when to record a show?"

I nodded.

"Well, the human body is like that VCR. But instead of a computer chip that sends out signals over wires, it has a brain that sends minute electrical impulses out over the nervous system."

"Does that mean that anyone can do what I can do?" I asked. "Anyone with a brain?"

"No," my mother said. "In most people those electrical impulses are very small, so small that they can only be detected by very sensitive equipment. You, on the other hand, grab energy from the world around you and store it in your body chemistry. Have you noticed any electrical devices acting strangely since your birthday?"

"Yes," I said. "Our car stalled, and my alarm

clock went dead. And the lights are always flickering and humming."

"Well, now you know what was really going
on," she said. "You pulled electricity out of those
machines and stored it for your own use."

"Is that how I'm able to shock people?"

My mother's eyes flashed with concern. "If
you're accidentally shocking people," she said,
"you need to learn to control your talent. If you're
not careful, the stored energy could lash out and
really hurt someone."

She took my hands in her own.

"In any case," she continued, "all that is just a side
effect of your true power. You're actually a jumper."

"A jumper?"

"Once you store enough power, you can create
a hole in the electromagnetic forces that govern
our reality. Jump through the hole and—*voilà*.
Instant time travel."

"Is that how you brought me back to 1989?" I
asked.

My mother smiled. "I didn't *bring* you here, Toni.
I'm not a jumper. You *came*. You brought yourself."

"But how? I wasn't even trying."

"You don't have to try. You do it instinctively."

"I don't understand."

"Look, sugar," my mother said, "when does a baby bird learn how to fly? Does it get lessons?"

"No," I replied.

"It's *born* knowing how to fly. It knows how to do it from the day it pecks out of the egg. But it's not until its mama pushes it out of the nest that it can actually spread its wings and take to the sky."

"What nest?" I asked, truly confused. "Are you saying I can fly?"

"Toni, listen to me. Getting pushed out of the nest—that's traumatic. When it happens, the bird suddenly 'remembers' how to fly. It's the same with you. I had to give you a little push. Then everything clicked into place."

"But," I started slowly, "how could you give me a push? Were you with me?"

"Sort of," my mother admitted. "Part of me was with you. You see, I planted a message in your brain a long time ago. I told it that when you saw something on your thirteenth birthday, you would come back to me, back to this time. Something bright and colorful that would stick out in your mind."

"The blouse . . . ," I whispered.

I *knew* I had seen it before!

"That's right," my mother said. "It's a visual trigger. Someday you'll be able to control your jumping skills. But this time you had to be pro-grammed." She checked her watch nervously. "Unfortunately we don't have much time."

Those were just the words I was dreading hear-ing. I was going to lose her. Again. "Why? What's going on?" I asked.

"Time traveling can be a very dangerous activity," she replied somberly. "It opens rifts in the space-time continuum. Even the simplest change made to the past can cause a horrible time quake to—"

She closed her eyes, shaking her head quickly as if shrugging off some bad memory. "It's very com-plicated, Toni. But the less time you spend here, the better. That's why I only programmed you to jump for fifteen minutes."

"Fifteen minutes! But—but I need more time with you! I just got here!"

Her grip on my hands tightened. "Listen to me, Toni. You have to find the others." She reached behind my desk and removed an envelope that had been taped in a hiding place on the wall. Opening the envelope, she removed a stack of photographs. The pictures were of five smiling, cute little kids. They looked to be about three or four years old.

"Look at these photographs," she said. "Do you recognize any of them?"

They did look a little familiar for some reason. Something about the eyes of one of them. But I didn't know anyone under the age of twelve, really. "No," I said. "They look kind of familiar, maybe . . . but not really."

"They'd be about your age by now," she persisted. "Their names might have been changed to protect their identities, but they were called Ethan, Elena, Todd, Ashley, and John."

I took the photo that seemed familiar from her and inspected it closely.

Yeah, it was definitely him—back when he was cuter and less destructive. "Not John," I corrected, "Jack. Jack Raynes. He's kind of a walking disaster, a total class clown. He goes to school with me." And now I recognized the other pictures. "So do Ethan Rogers and Ashley Rose," I added, pointing at two other photographs. "Todd Aldridge and Elena Vargas used to . . . but they've been missing for months."

My mother seemed disturbed by this news. She looked away, not meeting my eyes.

"What's wrong?" I asked.

"That means they know," she answered. "That means they'll be coming for you, too. Oh, my baby, I wish I could be there to protect you, but I can't. You're going to have to protect yourself."

"Protect myself from *who?*" I asked. She was really starting to frighten me.

Before she could answer, there was a tiny knock on the door. "Mom?" came a little girl's voice.

My mother went to the door and opened it. Braided hair with colorful barrettes, big brown eyes, more gums than teeth: I was shocked to find myself looking at my very own four-year-old self.

The little girl entered, smiling shyly up at me.

"Hey," I said to myself—my other self—"that's a very pretty dress you have on."

"Mommy?" the girl asked. "Who is the lady?"

"Her name is Antonia," my mother said.

"Antonia," the girl repeated. "Like me."

"That's right. Little Toni, meet Antonia."

"Hello," I said.

"Hello," she said at exactly the same instant.

Our mom crouched down next to the girl. "See the pretty lady's blouse?" she said, placing her fingertips on little Toni's temples. The four-year-old nodded, staring up at my shirt. "Remember what it looks like," my mother whispered in her ear.

I can't really explain what happened next. My mother's hands started to . . . *glow* from within. It looked like when you hold your hand over the end

72

of a flashlight except that the light kept getting brighter, whiter, until her hands looked as if they were made of neon. The light left her hands and seemed to enter little Toni's head. "Remember what it looks like," my mom said again.

The four-year-old's eyes gently closed, then re-opened, as if she had fallen asleep for a moment and was jerked back awake. I know the feeling; it happens to me all the time in math class. My mother put her hands on little Toni's shoulders. "Now, go downstairs and finish your drawing," she told the girl.

"Bye, Antonia," the little girl said to me.

"Good-bye, Toni," I replied.

Then she dashed out the door.

"What did you just do?" I asked my mom breathlessly.

"I just set the VCR," she replied simply. The lights overhead started to flicker. The now familiar humming was starting to rise. "We have less time than I hoped," she continued. "Listen to me, Antonia—"

But I wasn't listening. I had only instants left. Did she know what was going to happen to her? Did she know about the fire? If I told her, if I warned her, could she avoid that horrible morning?

73

If she did, if she lived, my entire childhood would have changed. I might have become a totally different person.

Can we alter our destiny? I wondered. *Or is the future set in stone, unchangeable?*

It didn't matter. I had to warn her.

"Mom, wait, listen. This is really important."

"What is it, sugar?"

"On July fifth there's going to be a fire in your office buil—"

She put her fingers on my lips, silencing me. "I don't want to know," she said. She shivered. "There's something I have to do, Toni, a place I have to go. I'll be gone for a long time."

"Take me with you, Mom," I said fiercely. "Wherever you're going—take me, too. I don't want to go on without you. I don't want to grow up without you. Wherever you're going, that's where I want to be."

"You can't come with me, my beautiful daughter," she replied sadly. "You have a job, too. You have to find Ethan, Ashley, and Jack. Don't waste any time. You have to use your powers to help them escape. And you have to survive."

"But I don't want to survive! I don't want to live without you!" I shouted.

"But part of me *is* with you, inside you," she said, holding me close. I buried my face on her shoulder, squeezed my eyes shut tight. "Use the powers of your mind, Antonia. Look inside yourself. If you do, you will always be able to see me."

I felt her let me go, but I kept my eyes closed. I inhaled deeply, smelling her perfume for what I knew would be the last time. Finally the spell was broken. I opened my eyes.

She was gone.

Chapter 7

I rushed from my bedroom and ran straight into my father, who was coming up the stairs. "Toni, did you just hear a strange humming noi—" His eyes swept down my body, then back up to my tearstained cheeks. "Toni, are you feeling all right? You look like you've been crying."

"I'm fine, Daddy," I said. "But from now on it's Antonia."

"I see," my father said skeptically. "Well, you have a visitor, *Antonia.*" He winked. "And it's a guy."

"Daddy!" I said.

The "guy" turned out to be the cute-but-dim Officer Dwayne Whaley. He was waiting for me in the kitchen, holding a cup of coffee.

"Officer Whaley needs to take you down to the police station to fill out some forms," my dad explained.

"Yeah, I just have to, uh, take you to the station," Dwayne repeated, "and, uh, fill out some forms."

Genius.

"Sure, that sounds fine," I said. But I remembered what my mother had said. I had a job to do—and that took priority over anything else. "Just let me go upstairs and change out of my nice new shirt."

"I wasn't sure why you were wearing it in the first place," my father said, giving me a curious look.

"Well," I said, giggling, "I just wanted to look my best for you menfolk."

It's amazing what you can get guys to believe if you compliment them and giggle.

"Go upstairs and change, then," my dad said. "We'll be right where you left us."

"I'll be right back," I replied.

As I headed up the stairs I could hear my father say, "That one's going to send a real shock through the community when she gets older."

I smiled to myself. *You have no idea*, I thought.

*   *   *

The first thing I did when I got upstairs was lock the door and pick up the phone—two things I can do in less time than it takes me to inhale. I called information, then dialed Ethan Rogers's number, hoping I didn't wind up talking to the chief of police with one of his officers waiting for me downstairs.

"Hello?" came Ethan's voice.

"Hi, Ethan. It's Antonia Douglas. You know, from school."

There was a pause on the other end. Then: "Toni? I heard about what happened last night. Listen to me. You're in extreme danger."

This wasn't at all what I expected. *I* was supposed to be warning *him*. "Danger?" I said.

"Yes, and there's more. I have some important information about the weird things that have been happening to you. We have to meet."

Why do boys always assume it's their job to make the plans? "Well," I replied, "my whole life has been weird lately."

"Believe me, I know," he said. "Look, don't tell anyone about what you can do. That's important. And meet me in the video arcade at the mall as soon as possible. I'll be waiting for you."

"Okay," I said, "but I won't be able to go for a little while."

"Why not? Your life may depend on it."

"Well, do you know one of your dad's men, Officer Dwayne Whaley?" I asked.

"Sure," he answered. "Really good at sports, really bad at coming up with original sentences. He bowls on my dad's team."

"He's here right now, waiting to take me to the station."

"The station?" Ethan asked. "Why?"

"He said I needed to fill out some forms."

"This could be a trap," Ethan said, a note of suspicion creeping into his voice. "Sometimes they disguise themselves as normal human beings."

"Sometimes *who* disguise themselves as normal human beings?" I demanded. I was getting frustrated. Why wouldn't anyone tell me what was going on?

"We can't talk about it over the phone. Just—I know this is going to sound crazy, but go ask Dwayne what his bowling average is."

"*What?*" I shouted, practically loud enough for my father to hear me downstairs.

"Toni," Ethan said, "this is serious."

"I am *not* going to go down there and ask him his bowling score. I have a reputation for sanity to protect, you know." *A reputation I am losing fast*, I added to myself.

"Bowling average, not bowling score. Antonia, he may be a killer. This is the only way we can be sure he is who he says he is."

Well, when you put it that way.

A moment later I popped back into the kitchen, still wearing the blouse. "Hi, Daddy," I said. "Officer Whaley, I was wondering . . . what's your bowling average?"

Officer Whaley gaped at me, surprised. "My bowling average?" he repeated.

"Yeah, your bowling average," I replied, trying to sound nonchalant. "You know, your *averagino de bowling-o?*"

"Two twenty-three," he answered.

"Thank you, Officer Whaley," I said.

"You're not changed yet?" Daddy asked.

"I'll be back in a minute," I said.

"She's at that age," I heard my father whisper to Officer Whaley as I headed back up the stairs.

I snatched the phone off the nightstand. "Two twenty-three," I said.

"Okay, it's him," Ethan said on the other end of the line. "He's safe."

"Was that really necessary?" I asked.

"Do you remember how I almost got killed, how Ashley was attacked out by the reservoir?" he asked.

"I'd heard rumors," I said.

"Both of those times it was because we trusted someone without checking them out thoroughly first. From now on, trust no one. Your survival depends on it. I'll see you at the mall."

There was a loud click as Ethan hung up. I stared at the silent receiver.

Does life get this serious for everyone at thirteen?

A few minutes later I was riding along in the back of a police cruiser. I couldn't believe how beautiful the day was. The air was fresh and sweet with the smell of newly mowed grass. Little League baseball was getting close to championship time; I could see some familiar faces practicing around the municipal field diamond. The sky was a perfect shade of blue. It seemed like there was no way that anything could go wrong on a day like today.

Which is what made me nervous.

Sitting in the back wasn't my idea. Officer Whaley said I had to for my own safety. Only police officers can sit up front. I slouched low, hoping no one would see me. After the whole shoplifting thing, all I needed was for someone to start saying they'd seen me in the back of a police car.

Because the backseat was made for criminals, it had no door handles, no buttons for the windows or locks, no way out. A thick grill of plastic and metal separated me from the driver's seat. I was starting to be glad that Ethan had made me check the young policeman out. It was almost as if I were in a little jail cell: I was totally at the mercy of whoever was sitting up front.

Officer Whaley wasn't much of a conversationalist—once you had covered bowling and football, there wasn't much else he had to say. After a few minutes my mind started to drift. I was anxious to talk to Ethan about what was going on. What secrets did he know?

For that matter, what did *I* know?

I tried to put together what little I had learned about my power. I remembered the way I felt so fizzy after sucking the energy out of the clock. I guess that was the same energy that I put into the stereo to make it play. So it seemed that I had to absorb energy first, and then I could unleash it.

"Everything okay back there?" Officer Whaley asked, hearing me laugh.

"Sure," I said. "I'm fine, Officer."

"Call me Dwayne. I'm going to take a little shortcut to the station," he announced. "It'll save us three-and-one-half minutes. I timed it."

"Great, Dwayne," I said.

We turned onto a small, abandoned road. And that's when we saw the body.

This time it was a real body, a human body, lying straight in the middle of the road. Officer Whaley slammed on the brakes. With a terrible squealing of tires, the car fishtailed. We spun around ninety degrees, stopping mere inches from running the poor guy over.

A week before, I probably would have fainted. Now I was merely curious.

"Holy moly," Officer Whaley said. "I think he's dead."

"What are we going to do?" I asked.

"You're going to just sit tight," he replied. "I'm going to go outside and investigate."

Before I could say another word, he pushed open the door and stepped outside the patrol car. Quickly he walked over to the fallen body.

I wondered if it was someone I'd known. It seemed like a middle-aged man of medium height and weight—maybe someone's father. I knew it was selfish, but all I could think was, *Thank God, it can't be my father—he's still back at home.* I tried to get a better look at the victim's face, but from my little cage inside the patrol car I couldn't make out anything at all.

Officer Whaley bent down, pressing a hand on the man's bloody neck. "I'm not getting a pulse," he muttered to himself. He reached into the car through the window and whipped the car radio from its holder. "Carla, this is Dwayne," he said. "Looks like we got a hit-and-run victim on Emmerson Road."

There are some moments in life that you think only happen in ghost stories and horror movies. I knew I was supposed to be beyond being shocked. But what happened next defied anything I could have been prepared for.

While Officer Whaley spoke into the microphone, the victim's body rose off the ground, silently and slowly, until it was sitting upright. As I watched, the bloody mass of pulp it had for a face writhed and pulsed, shifting shape. The shredded features wove together, seemed to heal. Soon the gruesome mask had morphed into an exact replica of Officer Whaley.

I totally lost it. I screamed at the top of my lungs. "Dwayne!" I yelled. "Look out!"

Officer Whaley spun around—toward me. "What?" he asked.

That was all the advantage his impostor needed. With a quick, hard blow to the neck, it knocked the young police officer out. As Officer Whaley started to fall to one side, unconscious, the shape-shifter deftly caught the microphone in one hand.

The car radio squawked. "Dwayne, this is Carla. Are you in some kind of trouble out there?"

The morpher looked me directly in the eye while speaking into the microphone. "Negative on that hit and run, Carla. It was just some guy asleep by the side of the road."

"Asleep, huh?" Carla asked.

"Yeah, my eyes must be playing tricks on me," the fake Dwayne continued, slipping into the driver's seat. He glanced at me in the rearview mirror. I could see his eyes. They had become flat black disks with no whites and no pupils. They seemed to suck the light out of the air around them. "Over and out," he concluded, and cut the microphone dead.

He stared at me through the rearview mirror. "You were a fool to demonstrate your powers in such a public place," he said. "You made it very easy to hunt you down."

My scream had washed some of my terror away. Now my temper was flaring up. "It's not nice to call other people names," I shot back. "How would you like it if someone called *you* a fool?"

"Called me a—?" he started to say.

"And *hello*," I continued, cutting him off. "As for 'hunting me down,' I was in the back of a locked patrol car. It's not like I had any means of *egress*," I said.

He stared at me blankly.

"It's a *vocabulary* word," I said. "Don't they have dictionaries where you come from?"

"You will join your friends in captivity," he snapped. "This will be the last ride of your life."

With that we took off down the road, siren blaring and lights flashing. This was bad. Very bad. I had to find some way out of the car.

Maybe I could jump out through the window when he stopped at an intersection. But I soon realized that wasn't going to happen. He was rolling right through the stoplights, increasing his speed with each passing minute.

I had to find some way to slow the car down, or I'd never get out alive. But how? If only the police cruiser would just stall out, like our Volvo did the night before.

With a shock of realization, I suddenly knew what had happened to the Volvo. It was like my mother explained: *I* had happened to it—me, the energy vacuum of Metier Junior High. When I was concentrating on the events of the day, I accidentally sucked the little Volvo dry.

I giggled as I realized what had happened to those punks: I had hit them with a car—the *electricity* of a car, anyway.

But could I do the same thing here, now that it really counted?

The impostor turned around when he heard my giggling. "You're laughing?" it asked. "Either you are incredibly brave or you do not realize the situation you are in."

"I realize the situation I'm in," I said. "But what *you* don't realize is that this baby bird just figured out how to fly."

"What does that mean?" he asked.

"Please," I said, "allow me to demonstrate."

I closed my eyes to concentrate and felt an impossibly wonderful rush as energy coursed into my body. It was as if I was falling through incredibly pure air from an amazing height, but there was no danger. I felt larger, grander, more imposing.

In an instant the police car's lights and siren went dead, like a candle someone had pinched out. Then the car engine stalled dead. We rolled to a stop right in the middle of the road.

The impostor whipped around to glare at me. "Turn this car back on," he snarled.

"Ooh," I said. "For a moment there I was scared."

"Restore my power now!" he shouted.

"You should really do something about your anger," I said. "It makes these little veins stand out on your forehead. *Very* unattractive."

"I have orders to take you alive," he said. "But they do not say that I cannot hurt you."

I glanced out the window. We were still on the back country road, and there wasn't another car in sight.

"I have five little words for you," I replied.

"What are they?"

"*Catch me if you can!*" I yelled, slamming both my hands on the door to the patrol car. With a burst of pink sparks and orange flame, the door exploded outward under the force of my pent-up energy. I dashed out of the smoldering car and into the woods, the fake officer in hot pursuit.

He was bigger, stronger, and faster than me. I knew he'd catch me in a matter of minutes unless I used my head. Again I gave silent thanks for the thousands of splits, leg lifts, and cartwheels that I'd done in cheerleading practice, which now gave me an extra burst of speed. Still, it would be useless unless I thought of something fast.

Up ahead was a chain-link fence with a sign posted: "State Watershed Area—No Trespassing." That was a start. I bet I could climb over it faster than any adult. With a hop, lift, and roll, I was up and over the fence. I hit the ground on the other side just as my pursuer reached the barrier.

He glared at me through the diamond-shaped holes. "Don't run from me," he snarled. "You're only wasting your energy."

As I was trying to think of a clever remark to yell back at him I had an idea. I turned and dashed into the woods.

Sure enough, a few instants later I heard him climbing the fence. There was no time to lose. I spun on my heels, ran back out of the forest, and made a beeline directly for the creature, now perched on top of the chain-link divide.

The expression of surprise on its face was priceless as I grabbed the fence directly underneath it.

"Looks like someone's in the hot seat," I said. With that I channeled the remaining energy from the car into the wire mesh of the fence. There was a giant flash as pinkish electricity crackled up the zigzag links. The creature screamed and fell off backward, hitting the ground hard. It lay there, motionless, on the other side of the fence.

I'd seen enough movies to know what to do then: run. Do not check to see if the monster is actually dead. Do not stop and pat yourself on the back. Run.

I kept running until I found myself at the reservoir, a wide, circular lake almost a half mile wide. I was exhausted. It's true, I had been running for almost thirty minutes, but I shouldn't have been as tired as I was. The only thing it could be was my power. When I used it, it drained me. It felt as if every time I let loose another electrical burst, a little bit of my life energy went with it.

I looked up at the sun, trying to get my bearings. It was no good. I had been a Girl Scout, but the only things I learned were how to sell cookies and sing camp songs. And, of course, that green is simply *not* my color. I wasn't sure where I was, but I knew I must be on the other side of the reservoir from the Metier Mall. Where Ethan was waiting. I had to get there somehow.

If only my legs would carry me.

Chapter 8

I arrived at the mall feeling like I had spent a week locked in a steam room—soaked with perspiration and barely able to stand. I thought I was going to collapse unless I found food. But then I realized that I wasn't hungry. I needed something else.

I needed to be *recharged*.

I staggered toward the entrance to the mall. By now the sun was low in the sky, throwing my long, twenty-foot shadow across the parking lot.

Was it already late afternoon? How long had I been running? It seemed like forever.

An ice-cream-slathered three-year-old was sitting on top of a coin-operated kiddie horse, crying his eyes out. Possibly because his quarter had run out, but more likely because he'd caught a glimpse of me.

I must have looked stunning: My hair was in full-on fright wig mode, my clothing was ripped and muddied, and I was walking like one of the zombies from *Night of the Living Dead*.

But I was beyond caring. I had made it to the mall; that was all that mattered. And now that I was there, I couldn't take another step. If Ethan wanted me to save his life, he was going to have to come outside and get me. Exhausted, I slumped against the nearest solid object.

Instantly I felt a flood of warm, fuzzy tingles traveling up my legs and over my tummy. My entire body felt like someone was giving me a luxurious Swedish massage. Even my hair felt better. And the sparks and flashes of blue light were beautiful to watch.

Hold the phone. *Sparks and flashes of blue light?* What was I inadvertently sucking the life out of *this* time?

I straightened up and realized that I was leaning on the coin box attached to the kiddie horse. Smoke was pouring out the sides and sparks were shooting out the base.

Meanwhile the horse was bucking and bouncing like crazy! It was all its little rider could do just to hang on. The machine wouldn't stop until I was done recharging. Then it died, never to be revived again.

"Again!" the toddler cried, clapping merrily.

"Sorry," I said. "One ride per customer."

I'm going to have to find a way to get this power thing under control, I thought, pushing into the air-conditioned mall and heading straight for the arcade.

I have to tell you, I have never understood why some people like video games. As far as I can tell, they're pointless. You shoot, you run, you blow things up—and then five minutes later you have to put in another quarter and start all over again. But there were at least a hundred machines in the arcade, and more than half of them had kids waiting in line to get their turn at the controls.

It wasn't too hard to find Ethan. He was sitting in one of those two-player racing car games, a dorky *X-Men* knapsack nestled in his lap. From the looks of him, he'd been there all afternoon—and probably would have been happy to wait a few hours longer.

I knocked on the cockpit window. "Is this seat taken?" I asked.

He grinned back at me, but his smile turned into a look of horror as he took in my appearance. I had almost forgotten that I had just been chased by a creature with two black disks for eyes.

Apparently it showed.

"What happened?" he whispered, speaking just loudly enough to be heard over the din of the dozens of competing video games.

"You were right about my life being in danger." I was surprised by the lack of emotion in my voice. Either I was in shock or I was getting used to this.

"Was it Dwayne?" he asked.

"No," I replied. "Just some guy we met along the way."

"Have a seat," he said. "If it looks like we're just playing a video game, they won't pay any attention to us. Have you ever played Twisted Metal III before?"

"Not really," I answered.

"It's a lot like driving a car," he told me.

"*Hello,*" I responded, "I'm, like, three years from my learner's permit."

"Well, consider this an advance on your education," he said. "And as a bonus you learn how to run *over* things."

A lesson, I realized, that might actually come in handy.

He slid a few tokens into the slot, and we began to play the game. "When did you first start noticing there was something strange going on?" he asked.

"Just last night," I replied, "when I time-traveled for the first time."

"Time-traveled?" he asked, surprised. "I didn't hear anything about that. All I heard was how you practically electrocuted a gang of punks."

"Well," I said, "let's just say it was a birthday I'll never forget. I'll tell you all about it, but first—who's after me? Why is my life in danger?"

Ethan proceeded to tell me all about what had really been going on in my little hometown. If you've ever seen the movie *Men in Black*, it's not so different from that. For almost a year Metier had been a nonstop battlefield in the war between aliens and humans. But only a few of us had any idea that anything out of the ordinary was going on. I guess that old saying is true: Most people look but do not see. The clues were all there, but no one had put them together.

First Todd Aldridge was abducted last August. He had gone out to the reservoir to try out a camera he'd gotten for his thirteenth birthday. The camera was recovered, but the film was never found. Apparently something didn't like having its picture taken.

Ethan discovered he had superhuman fighting ability on the day of his thirteenth birthday, in

October. A few days later he used his talents to stop a robbery—right in front of the store's security camera. The video of five-foot-one, eighty-pound Ethan punching, tripping, gouging, and kicking the daylights out of the armed burglar was replayed on the TV news. A few days later an alien assassin paid him a visit—disguised as the local news anchorman. Ethan had to battle the assassin to the death just to escape with his life.

As soon as your powers blossom, Ethan told me, the alien assassins will try to hunt you down. It's a race against time. They can take on the shape of any human being—a janitor, a police officer, or your best friend. One alien even took on the form of Todd Aldridge and almost lured the entire group to their death. Fortunately the alien imitated Todd a little *too* closely, duplicating the missing boy's humanity and compassion. When it came to the moment of truth, the impostor helped his human friends to escape.

I was barely paying attention to the video game that was bleeping and flashing in front of my face. I thought that after the events of the past twenty-four hours, nothing would ever surprise me again. But I was stunned. How could this incredible story be true? It meant that I would never be able to live a normal life—not until we won the battle.

"Some of us were lucky and found safety in numbers," Ethan continued. "Others, like Elena, weren't so fortunate. Unless we stick together, we don't have a chance. It's time you met the rest of the team."

"Ashley Rose and Jack Raynes," I said.

"At your service," said Jack, stepping out from behind a Mortal Kombat III with his skateboard in hand. He wore a baseball cap turned around backward in that way guys do when they think they're cool, and he had dark sunglasses on—even though we were in a dark room inside a mall. "How's the little cheerleader today?" he quipped.

"Jack, don't be obnoxious," Ashley said, suddenly appearing at his side. "Not that you can help it." She wore her trademark dyed-black sweater over black jeans and black combat boots, even though it was June and ninety degrees out. I suppressed a little giggle. We must have looked like a support group for the fashion impaired.

"So what can *you* guys do?" I asked.

"Instant translation," Jack replied. "You say it, I spray it. Now serving French, Spanish, German, Malay, Sanskrit, Tonga-Tonga, and let's not forget Braille, insect, and fax machine."

"Jack is a little modesty challenged," Ashley apologized.

"How about you, Ashley?" I asked. Ashley had always been kind of an outcast at school—she only had maybe one real friend, she dressed like something from late night MTV, and none of the boys liked her. After she almost drowned in the Metier Reservoir last October, we even started calling her Splashly Rose. But now that I was actually face-to-face with her, I felt bad about the way I'd treated her in the past. Underneath it all, I saw, she was actually kind of pretty—and clearly a lot cooler than Jack Raynes. "What can *you* do?"

"It's kind of hard to describe," Ashley said, blushing. I could see she didn't really like being the center of attention. "I can swim underwater for as long as I want. I could probably live at the bottom of the ocean. But my real talent is stranger. I can . . . split myself in half. Like a planarian." She paused expectantly. "A planarian is—"

"—a small, nonsegmented flatworm that can be divided without injury," I concluded.

"That's right!" Ashley beamed. "Hardly anyone knows that!"

"It's a vocabulary word," I confided. We grinned conspiratorially. I had found a friend.

"So we've all got superpowers," I summed up, "but why? Why is this going on? Why are these aliens coming after us? And why Metier?"

Ethan frowned. "We don't really know that, despite all the research we've done. All we've been able to put together is that it has something to do with our parents."

"How do you mean?" I asked.

"All of us grew up without a parent," Ethan answered. "Well, except me. I grew up without either biological parent. I was adopted."

"So Chief Rogers isn't your real father?" I asked. Now that I thought about it, it wasn't so surprising. The athletic police chief and the scrawny boy standing in front of me couldn't have been more different, but I'd never put two and two together.

"That's right," he replied, "although he's always tried to treat me as if I were his real son. All of our missing biological parents died or vanished right around the same day."

"July fifth," I replied automatically.

"That's right," Ethan said.

"Do you think there's a chance they're not actually dead?" I asked, hope suddenly flaring up inside me.

"I don't know," Ethan answered, flustered. "I guess it's possible."

"I wish I'd asked her this morning," I said suddenly.

"Asked who, Toni?" Ashley asked.

"My mother. That's part of my power—if I can store enough energy, I can travel through time. Or at least I will be able to once I've learned how to do it on my own. This time my mother had to program me."

I looked from face to face, thinking, *Is any of this making sense? Or do you think I'm cracked?* But apparently they were used to hearing stories like mine because none of them seemed in the least bit surprised.

"So you actually traveled back in time?" Ethan asked.

"Yes. I could only stay for a few minutes—I wanted to stay longer, but she told me it was dangerous. That we both had jobs to do."

"And then what happened?" Ethan wanted to know.

"Well, then I was back in the present, and Officer Whaley was waiting for me, and—oh no!"

"What's wrong?" Ashley asked.

"Officer Whaley! The assassin they sent for me knocked him unconscious in the middle of the road. He's probably still there!"

"You just left the guy lying there, bleeding?" Jack asked. "Boy, remind me never to get knocked unconscious around you."

"Well, *excuse* me," I shot back, "I was locked in a patrol car being driven by a bug-eyed freak from outer space. I didn't have a big say in the matter."

"Guys, come on," Ethan said. "Fighting isn't going to make things better. There's someone who needs our help. We can call an ambulance from the pay phones by the food court."

I hoped that Officer Whaley was all right. I realized that Jack's words only stung because he was telling the truth: I never once thought about going back to save the fallen officer. If anything happened to him, it would be my fault.

Ethan picked up the phone receiver and dialed. "Nine-one-one," the voice on the other end of the line said. "Emergency services. Please describe your emergency."

"There's an officer down," Ethan said, trying to sound like an adult. "You can find him at . . ." He looked at me, questioning.

"Emmerson Road," I prompted.

"Emmerson Road," Ethan said. The operator said something to Ethan, causing him to turn to me again. "Where on Emmerson Road is he?" he asked.

"Tell her by the fork to Winnetka Lane," I said.

"By the fork to—," Ethan started to say. Then

he stopped suddenly and looked at the receiver. "That's funny," he said. "She hung up."

He replaced the phone in its cradle and picked it up again. "No dial tone," he said, concerned. He picked up another phone, listened. "This one's dead, too. The phone lines have been cut."

"This is what always happens in a suspense film," Ashley said, "right before the lights go out."

As if on cue, the mall's large overhead lights began going out one after the other.

"Are *you* doing this?" Jack demanded of me.

"No," I replied. "It's not me."

In less than a minute the mall was plunged into darkness. The only light came from the high glass ceiling over the food court, and it wasn't much. By now the sun had set, and the pink-orange twilight was rapidly fading to a blue-gray dusk. The rest of the mall was concealed in deep, pitch-black shadow. Ordinarily I would have been freaked, but now that I was with my friends, I didn't feel frightened at all.

"I guess it's just a blackout," Ashley said.

"Yeah, right," Jack replied, taking off his sunglasses. "Like anything normal ever happens in our lives."

Mall goers milled about with nervous looks on their faces. Storekeepers rapidly shut their doors to guard against looting, rushing everyone out into the mall corridors. The halls were already jam-packed with anxious-looking shoppers. In a minute people were going to start panicking.

"Watch. In about ten seconds the alien mother ship is going to drop anchor right on top of the food court."

"Jack, stop trying to scare the girls," Ethan said.

"Yeah, Jack," I said, "because the girls aren't getting scared."

His eyes widened. "The beauty queen speaks," he said. He made a little half bow. "Fine, Your Majesty. Whatever you say."

I should have been mad, but something about the way he said it reminded me of how Han Solo spoke to Princess Leia in *Star Wars*.

You know, Jack, I wanted to say, *you look a lot better with the lights out.* Instead I just smiled at him. Jack looked back at me, baffled. Then he grinned, too.

The voices of concerned mall shoppers were getting louder and louder. Just as it looked like we might be in for a full-scale stampede, four security guards appeared on the scene. In their black shirts, black pants, and black baseball caps they blended neatly into the darkness. Fortunately they were carrying flashlights. "This way, please," one of them shouted over the din of frightened voices.

"Nothing to worry about. No reason to be alarmed. Let's keep it moving."

The four men started directing traffic toward the main exit. The crowd responded quickly, forming a hasty line up to where the guards stood. We walked over to the back of the line.

"See, Jack?" I teased. "It's just a power outage. Nothing to be frightened of. Are you feeling any better?"

"*Don't trust anyone,*" Jack answered, "particularly if that person is a grown man wearing a baseball cap. Look."

He was pointing at the security men. As each shopper passed, a guard shone his flashlight in their face, then waved them on.

"They're looking for someone," Ethan said.

"Bingo," Jack replied.

"Four guards equals four mutant kids," Ashley said. "They're looking for *us.*"

"So you think they're . . . aliens?" I asked, still trying to deal with the reality of the situation.

"Look how they're still wearing sunglasses, even though it's supposed to be the middle of a power outage," Ethan said.

"Yep," Jack answered, pointing to his eyes. "Black disk city."

"We have to find a way out of here without drawing attention to ourselves," Ethan said. "Let's drift back in the direction we came from and try to find a store that's still open."

"But it's dark back there!" I complained. "What if there are more security guards behind us? How can we be sure we aren't walking right into an ambush?" I didn't want to whine, but if they were wrong and those were *real* security guards who remembered me from the previous night—*and* they caught me in a store in the middle of a blackout—I was going to be in more trouble than anyone in the history of Metier Junior High.

Besides, I think whining may just be nature's response to being chased through your hometown mall by aliens.

"I can use my heat vision to see in the dark," Ethan said. "All we have to do is find a store that has a door that lowers electronically. It won't have closed during the power outage. We can slip inside and hide."

"The new Nike Town," I said instantly. "The doors close automatically at eight-thirty and don't reopen until nine the next morning." Who says shopping isn't educational?

We were just in time. The last of the mall goers

were safely escorted out. Trying not to draw attention to ourselves, we turned and headed back down the corridor toward the Nike outlet.

"Are they watching us?" I asked Ethan.

"I don't know," he whispered back. "I'm scanning the corridor ahead of us for a trap."

Jack looked back over his shoulder. "Well, if they weren't watching us before," he said, "they sure are now."

I glanced back at the four guards. One of them was pointing his flashlight toward us and saying something to the others.

"I have a new vocabulary word for all of us," I announced.

"What is it?" Ashley asked.

"*Run,*" I said.

Chapter 9

Escape wasn't going to be easy.

The alien guards were running toward the high-tech shoe store, flashlights in their hands. "I know they aren't human," I panted as we wove through the racks of sports clothing, "but I'm still amazed at how fast they move."

"And keep in mind," Ashley added, "they all have heat vision and enhanced senses of smell and hearing."

"It's no good," Ethan said. "They know we're here. We can't get out. It's only a matter of time before they catch us. We have to think of an alternate plan."

"Well, I can buy us some time," I volunteered. "But I'm going to be cranky afterward."

*   *   *

With an enormous *crash!* the gates to Nike Town slammed shut. I had channeled some of the energy sucked from the kiddie horse into the twin motors driving Nike Town's security gate. Now the heavy metal barrier stood firmly between us and the aliens.

"Keep moving," Ethan shouted. "Head toward the back of the store."

"They'll be through that door in a matter of minutes," Jack said as he ran. "We need a plan."

"Are you kidding?" I asked, incredulous. "That door is a foot thick and fifteen feet high. That's, like, a million-dollar door."

"Unfortunately," Ashley responded, "Jack's right—for once. We've got maybe two minutes. Three, tops."

Ethan turned to me. "Toni, you know this store. Is there a rear exit, a changing room, anything?"

"On this level? No—and the escalators are way back toward the entrance," I answered.

"We can't head back that way. It's too risky," Ethan replied.

I racked my brain. *There's no exit. No changing rooms. But there* is *a way out.* I was sure of it. It was on the tip of my tongue—so what was it? Then it hit me. "The shoe elevator!" I shouted.

"The what?" Jack asked.

"It's like a dumbwaiter that brings you your shoes," I explained.

"They've got an elevator just for shoes?" Ashley asked.

"Yep, and it's totally *fab*," I told her as we ran. "You order the shoe you want and in a few minutes it appears on this cute minielevator."

"That's too cool," Ashley said.

"Okay," Jack said, annoyed, "we're fleeing, not shopping. What does this elevator have to do with anything?"

Honestly, boys just do not understand the importance of good shoes. *"Do the math,"* I explained. "If it brings up shoes, it must lead down to the storage level."

"Will it hold our weight?" Ashley asked.

"Probably not, if it's meant for sneakers," Ethan said, "but if we can somehow remove the elevator itself, the shaft is a straight shot to freedom."

"Let's do it," Ashley and I said simultaneously.

Finding the elevator was easy. Yanking the tiny elevator car, still laden with footwear, out of the small shaft was harder.

Just as the contraption pulled free the floor shook under a violent crash from behind us.

Something had just fallen. Something a foot thick and fifteen feet high, from the sound of it.

"I think the million-dollar door has just been marked down," Jack said.

"*Knocked* down is more like it," Ethan responded.

For a second we just stared at the tiny square opening before us. The hole looked big enough for a person to fit down—barely.

The sound of the guards' footsteps snapped us into action.

"I'll go first," Jack whispered, "and see if it's safe."

"When you hit bottom, don't stop to wait for the rest of us," Ethan whispered back. "Hit the ground running. It's smarter if we split up, anyway."

Maybe it was smarter. But it also meant that in a few moments I would be alone. In the dark.

Well, not totally alone. There were always the aliens to think about.

Moments later I was slipping and sliding down the elevator shaft, hands firmly pressed against the sheet metal walls to avoid plummeting twenty feet to the ground. I've just got this to say: I'm glad I'm not claustrophobic, and I'm glad that I'm in good shape. The metal chamber was meant for athletic shoes, not athletic thirteen-year-olds. It felt like a vertical coffin.

I was the last person to arrive in the stockroom. I could hear the alien guards tearing apart the upper level, looking for us. It was only a matter of time before they found the elevator shaft and realized where we'd gone to. And once they did— they'd be wriggling down after us.

"Ethan?" I whispered into the darkness. "Ashley? Jack?"

There was no answer. I guess they'd gone ahead with the plan and taken off their separate ways.

I took a deep, shuddering breath. I suppose we made a more difficult target if we split up, but a part of me was worried. Whatever happened to safety in numbers?

I reached out, feeling my way past the shelves and shelves of shoe boxes, until my hand brushed the bar of a fire door. I pushed it open as quietly as possible and found myself back out in the mall.

The lower level seemed even darker than the upper level had been. Though I didn't have Ethan's heat vision, I *had* spent many hours here with a credit card as my guide. Finding my way around would be no problem.

113

But where should I go?

No matter where I ran in the mall, I knew, the aliens would find me sooner or later. They would methodically comb both levels until they found me. And they probably had more "guards" waiting at the exits. Trying to get away seemed impossible.

Unless, I thought, *I can get away without actually leaving the building*.

My mind whirled.

If I could use my time-jumping abilities, they'd have no way to follow me. Then it would be *cake* to walk out of the mall—nine years before they thought to start looking for me. But I still didn't know how to time travel on my own. I didn't even know where to begin.

If only I had that blouse, I thought, I could activate my "programming" and travel back to 1989. But the blouse was out of reach, at home. And it was a one-of-a-kind designer item: There was no sense looking for it in Boutique Chic, even if I could get to the Snob Palace without being detected by my alien pursuers.

I bit my lip, discouraged. I needed that blouse to complete the mental picture—to be my "visual trigger," as my mom had put it. Without it, I had no hope of escape.

Wait a second. If I needed a *mental* picture . . . maybe an *actual* picture would do the trick!

The front entrance to the mall was just down the corridor, looking like a light gray square in the blackness. I slipped off my shoes and padded quietly toward it, keeping low to the ground. Sure enough, as I drew closer I could make out the shadowy figure of an alien guard watching the exit. Luckily he didn't seem to notice me as I crept over to the Wall of Shame.

I slid behind the counter of the information kiosk. Then, as silently as possible, I reached up my hand, untacking my photo from the rogues' gallery of shoplifters and vandals. I could have kissed the security guy who put my picture up there—well, okay, maybe not *kissed* him, but I would have given him a pretty good squeeze.

It was too dark to view the picture from where I was crouched behind the counter. I slowly rose, holding the Polaroid up to the dim light that filtered through the glass doors. I could just barely make it out now. There I was, wearing the blouse, looking like I did in my mind's eye. I studied the picture, concentrating as hard as I could. Soon the weird feeling of déjà vu set in, causing the hair on my neck to raise.

Was it working?

As if in answer, a loud humming started to emanate from the ceiling—

Just as the guard looked up and spotted me.

"Target in sight!" he growled into his walkie-talkie.

He was less than twenty yards away and closing fast. There was no escape. No exit—except for the one in my mind, that is. And I didn't know if that door would open.

I held the picture tightly. It took every ounce of courage to shut my eyes when I knew that sudden death was rushing straight for me. But sometimes you have to have faith.

The humming grew louder and louder, building to a fever pitch. Just as it reached its climax I felt a cold, viselike hand grab my wrist.

"You have been captured," rasped a cold, inhuman voice in front of me. I opened my eyes. The guard had removed his dark sunglasses. The flashlight in his hand cast an eerie glow on his evil, hollow-eyed face. *You are ours.*

"I have a question for you," I said, giving him my best "please don't hurt me, Mr. Big Alien" look.

"What is it?" the guard asked.

"Doesn't it *suck* being *wrong* all the time?" I shouted, wrenching my arm from his iron grasp.

His expression was priceless, but I only got to see it for an instant before the lights went out.

Or rather, before they came *on*.

Because suddenly I materialized—if that's what you call it—in broad daylight, right in the middle of a pack of shoppers. They didn't even seem to notice me. I understood the feeling. When I'm on a shopping rampage, nothing short of an actual plane crash will distract me—and even then, it had better be a pretty big plane.

I looked around the mall, thinking that no matter how many times I did this, I'd still be weirded out. A New Kids on the Block song was playing in the Sam Goody. I gawked at the old shops and bizarre, late eighties styles. Can you believe we ever thought that parachute pants were cool?

I was having second thoughts about my plan to leave the mall. Sure, it would be easy to walk outside, then rematerialize a safe distance away in 1998. But what good would it do? Back in the future, Ethan and the others were probably still trapped inside. I had to find some way to help them. And I only had fifteen minutes to figure out how.

First things first. I walked into Sears and

strode purposefully to the counter. The clerk was a little surprised to see someone dressed for June instead of December, but I gave him my most heart-stopping smile, the one I normally reserve for getting my allowance raised. It was all the poor man could do to smile back.

"Hello." I beamed, twirling a strand of hair around my finger. "I'm looking for a present for my father. Something *powerful* and *electric.*"

Sears never knew what hit it.

Moments later I tottered out of Sears, leaving the poor salesclerk to wonder why every television and stereo in the electronics section had suddenly gone dead.

As I hurried along the corridor I tried to keep from actually levitating off the ground. I felt like I had just gotten the best makeover of my life. Little bursts of energy fluttered and exploded in my tummy like butterflies with the hiccups.

I was ready to tangle with some aliens.

What could I bring back that might help me? I scanned the mall, looking for something to inspire me. But all I saw were shoppers, more shoppers, and a snowman handing out flyers.

Wait a second. *A snowman handing out flyers?*

I walked over and took one from him. Yes, it was the same flyer I'd gotten yesterday. But without any writing on the back.

Then I remembered how the handwriting had looked so familiar. My skin crawled with goose bumps.

Could it be . . . ?

When I looked over in the direction of Boutique Chic, I saw the most startling thing yet: There *I* was, getting thrown out by Paula, the Witch of the West.

I have to tell you, it's one thing to know you have attitude. It's another to see it in motion. I wanted to applaud myself as I heard my double tell the stuck-up saleslady: "It's a vocabulary word. Look it up!"

There was no time to waste. "Hey," I told Snowboy, "can you help me play a practical joke on my, er, twin sister?"

"Sure," he said in a squeaky, trembling voice. Either my good mood was reflected in my looks, or he was deep into puberty. "What is it?"

"Do you have a pen?" I asked.

A few minutes later, as I watched him walk away with the flyer in his hand, I could have hit myself for not writing something more practical than the note about the cake. *Don't get in the police car,* for example, or, *Stay in bed tomorrow.* But if I had, would I have been able to get away from the punks? I suppose some things were just meant to be.

My time was almost up. I had mere moments left before I'd be zapped back to the blacked-out mall. What was I going to do to defend myself? Where could I arm myself against an entire posse of aliens?

There was only one answer. I knew I had to hurry. The clock was ticking down.

Luckily for me, KidsLand Toys wasn't too crowded. I rushed toward the back of the store, selecting the items I'd need. In no time my basket was overflowing with merchandise.

My shopping spree was almost done, but I still had one item left. To my dismay, there were no Ultra Soaker water guns left on the rack. I looked around, hoping one had been put on the wrong shelf. Then I spotted an eight-year-old with one of the big, neon green, double-barreled rifles.

"Can I see that for a second?" I asked, prying it out of his hands.

"But—!" he started to say, looking as if he might cry.

"Trust me, kid," I replied, "I need this more than you."

Just then I felt a tap on my shoulder. I turned to face the store manager, a weasely-looking guy with a thin mustache and an ugly maroon vest. "Shopping for a friend?" he asked, frowning, looking at the dozens of boxes clutched in my arms.

"No," I replied sweetly. I cast a nervous glance up at the ceiling. The lights above were bright and steady.

"For yourself?" the manager asked, tweaking his mustache between two fingers.

"Not exactly," I answered, still as sweet. *Come on, start humming*, I silently ordered.

"Then can I ask what you're doing with all those items?" he hissed.

"Just . . . waiting," I replied.

"Waiting *for what?*" he demanded, clearly out of patience.

"My exit cue," I answered as the fluorescents started flashing and the low humming noise started resounding overhead. I tucked the Ultra Soaker under my arm, clutched the basket to my side, and darted past the startled manager. I dashed out into the mall—right through the shoplifting detectors.

"*Stop that gir—!*" I heard the manager shout behind me as the store alarm went off.

But then the lights went out, and I had bigger problems to worry about.

_____ **Chapter 10**

When I turned around, KidsLand was dark and silent, locked behind a metal gate. No sign of an angry store manager. No signs of anything, in fact. I anxiously scanned the dark corridor. Where were Ethan, Ashley, and Jack? Had they escaped?

A few minutes later I realized that my fears had come true. They hadn't gotten out. I could hear the sounds of a struggle in the darkness ahead of me— coming from the direction of the food court. From the sound of it, my friends were fighting for their lives.

Go, guys, I silently prayed. *Kick some alien butt!*

I raced toward the food court, pausing only to dunk the Ultra Soaker in the large fountain outside The Nature Company. Once both barrels were full, I continued as quickly as I could under my heavy load of stolen merchandise. I promised myself I'd return it when this was all over. Despite all the rumors, I was not and never will be a shoplifter.

When I was still a few hundred yards away, I felt the entire mall start to tremble under the force of an enormous vibration. At first I thought it was some monster plane passing overhead, then I decided it had to be an earthquake. But this was Wisconsin! What was going on?

When I reached the food court, I found out.

Tables and chairs were strewn in a haphazard mess down the center of the large central eating area. It was easy to guess the path my friends had taken to escape their pursuers.

Or rather, to *not* escape. For there, at the far end of the food court, were Ethan, Jack, and Ashley, their arms pinned tightly behind their backs by the four alien guards. They weren't even struggling anymore, just looking up toward the glass ceiling with awed expressions.

I followed their gaze up to the skylight and felt my own physiognamy assume the countenance of incredulity.

In other words, my mouth fell open.

Because there it was. The mother ship. Landing on the food court. Just like Jack had predicted.

With a brain-shattering *crash!* the alien craft broke through the massive glass skylight and slowly lowered itself down into the building. Shards of glass and metal rained down as the plastic tables were vaporized by the enormous propulsion jets underneath the ship. The new Cinna-Buns stand burst into flames. I flattened myself against the wall as a hot wind whipped at my face. I couldn't believe what I was watching: A UFO was actually landing in my mall.

Six spidery metal legs touched down on the scorched floor. Almost at once a brilliant white line cracked in the underside of the gleaming metal craft. It widened to disclose a hatchway beyond. A kind of gangplank descended from within, noiselessly settling on the ground.

An instant later an alien emerged from the craft. It was the first time I'd seen one in its true form: tall and skeletal, its two large, horrible eyes shining like black fire in its large, pale white head. He—if it *was* a he—was dressed in a shimmery silver tunic and clutched some sort of crystal scepter in one hand. I guessed he was the leader. And I guess I guessed correctly—because the next thing he did was order the "guards" to take my friends on board the craft.

My heart plummeted as Ethan, Jack, and Ashley

were forced up the gangway and into the craft. What were the aliens going to do to them?

The lead alien waited until they had disappeared inside the ship. Then he turned and shouted into the darkness: "Antonia Douglas! Show yourself! If you do not come out of hiding, I will kill your friends!"

Riiight. Me—give up without a fight. Like *that* was gonna happen.

"How do I know that if I give myself up, you won't kill us all, anyway?" I shouted from my hiding place.

The leader's head instantly snapped in my direction. I ducked back behind a garbage container, hoping his alien heat vision didn't extend this far.

"Our orders have changed," the alien answered smoothly. "We are to bring you back alive—if possible. It's your choice. We can bring back four live captives . . . or three dead bodies. You decide."

I gulped hard. It was moment-of-truth time. I stepped out of the shadows, my hands raised over my head. "Here I am," I announced.

"Smart girl," the leader pronounced. He took a step toward me, holding out his scepter like a gun. "Very smart girl. You're saving your friends' lives."

I stared my opponent straight in the eye. He was a good two heads taller than me, but I knew I could take him. I was younger. Quicker. And I'd come to the battle prepared.

He was going *down*.

I closed my eyes. Not because I was scared.

Because I was concentrating.

Instantly the air was filled with the sound of sirens—police sirens. A dozen police cars screamed across the floor of the food court from all directions.

Of course, they were only toys. Grasshopper IIs, to be exact—fast little suckers that can do seventy miles per hour on a nine-volt battery. But you should have seen them on Toni power. It wasn't exactly the cavalry, but it gave me the few seconds I needed.

The alien leader was distracted, trying to figure out just what was running around his feet at rocket speed. I dashed back across the pavilion to my hiding place, where I had planted another secret weapon.

"Stand back," I said, pointing the firearm at the leader, "or things are going to get nasty."

The leader hesitated, then peered closely at the object in my hands. "That is a mere toy," he announced. "It will not save you." He started to walk toward me.

I pulled the trigger, letting him have it.

A crystal stream of water sluiced through the air, leaving my opponent dripping wet. He spat water out of his mouth, then patted down his uniform. "Stupid girl," he said, standing in a long, narrow puddle that stretched to my feet. "Did you think water would make me melt?" He clucked his tongue in mock sympathy.

"Melt?" I asked innocently. "Nope. I was thinking more like . . . *fry!*"

Kneeling down, I slammed my hands into the trail of water connecting us. Instantly crackling threads of pink electricity ran through the puddle and over the alien's body, engulfing him in a deadly electric glow. He thrashed in place, shaking like a Tickle Me Elmo doll, before stumbling to one side and collapsing in a heap.

"Who's next?" I asked as the four alien guards poured out of the UFO, rushing at me from all sides. I waited until they were close enough, then pulled out secret weapon number two. "Anyone like to play Slinky?" I said. With that I whipped two of the metal springs in an electrified arc over my head. They lashed out like two lethal Chinese yo-yos.

Seconds later there were four more unconscious aliens on the floor.

You remember my motto: When the monster is down, *run.* The only question was, To where? If I left the mall to get help, the aliens might wake up while I was gone and escape, taking my three friends with them. I couldn't let that happen. But if I didn't want to leave, the only other place to run was . . .

I glared at the enormous metal disk crouching above the former Hot-Dog-on-a-Stick stand, as if *it* was somehow the enemy instead of the aliens who had built it. It looked like a giant metal beetle. Was I really mental enough to try what I had in mind? I knew what the answer was:

Yes, I'm just that mental.

Two seconds later I scurried up the gangway and into the alien ship.

The interior of the spacecraft was disappointing.

All I can say is, if I had to spend as much time in one place as those aliens probably had to spend inside that UFO, I would have gotten out a catalog and spent some serious cash on interior design. I kid you not. It looked like they had thrown it all together at the last minute. I mean, if you owned a spaceship, would *you* want it to look like a *garage?* The only neat space was the ship's ceiling: a gleaming white dome that seemed to crackle like the static on a television screen.

The first thing I did was close the hatchway behind me. There was a kind of switch on the wall where you entered. I ran my hand across it. The gangway rose and the metal doors slid—hissing—into place.

The Thrilling Threesome weren't hard to find. Ethan, Ashley, and Jack were standing upright, each trapped in a formfitting tube of clear yellow plastic that stretched from floor to ceiling—not the most flattering look, I assure you. Ashley's eyes followed me as I crossed the round chamber, but the rest of her was fixed in place, like one of those creepy paintings they have at haunted houses.

It was too horrible for words—my friends had been turned into human cannelloni! I had to get them out. Fortunately my luck held. The very first control I tried activated the release mechanism. With a *whoosh* the tubes were sliding up and off my friends. I was worried they would be drugged or semiconscious, but then I heard Jack say as the plastic slid up over his mouth, "Gee, thanks. Could you have waited *any longer?*"

"Oops," I shot back, "I'm sorry. I was looking for a way to free just Ethan and Ashley. Jack, why don't you be a good boy and get back in your tube?"

"Nice going, Toni," said Ashley, shaking the cramps out of her arms. "I knew you'd come through."

"What's the alien situation?" Ethan wanted to know. "Are we in danger?"

"Not at the moment," I replied.

"What happened?" Ethan asked. "How did you get on the ship?"

"I fought the aliens," I answered, "and I won."

"Oh, come on." Jack snorted. "Are you trying to tell me that a girl like you killed five aliens?"

"Well . . . yeah," I replied proudly. "Kind of."

"Kind of?" Ethan asked.

"Come on," Ashley interrupted, "we can talk about that later. Let's get out of here."

We ran for the port. I ran my hand across the weird switch again, and the large metal doors hissed open.

Revealing five very irate aliens standing below.

I quickly ran my hand back over the switch.

"I thought you said you *killed* the aliens," Ethan squeaked as the doors slid back into place.

"Okay. So maybe I just *stunned* them," I replied.

"Well, maybe you should remind them that they're supposed to be stunned," Jack said sarcastically, "because it looks to me like you merely ticked them off."

Suddenly the ship started vibrating under what sounded like hammer blows. The aliens were trying to break through the hull of the ship. I had a sudden feeling of déjà vu—this was just like being attacked by that gang of punks. Except this time, I thought, it was going to take more than birthday cake to stop them.

"They know this ship better than we do," Ethan said. "They'll find a way in if we just sit here and wait."

"So what can we do?" I asked.

"Fly the ship," Jack responded smugly.

"Oh yeah, right," I sniped. "I bet you couldn't fly a paper airplane."

"I've played Flight Simulator enough," he shot back, "plus I can read the alien writing on the controls. And besides, it's not like we have another choice, princess."

I knew he was right. Either the impossible happened and our class clown flew a spaceship out of the food court, or we were all dead.

"Okay, Jack," Ethan said, "why don't you go for it?"

Instants later Ethan, Ashley, and I braced ourselves against the walls of the spacecraft, holding on to anything that looked solid, while Jack strapped himself into a seat at the controls. The aliens' hammering was so intense by now that it sounded as if it was coming from inside the ship. I knew we didn't have much time—soon they would have damaged the ship so badly that it might never be able to leave the ground. It would be destroyed by the forces of liftoff.

"Are you ready?" Jack hollered over the terrible pounding noise. "Here we go!"

He placed his hands on the alien controls—not a keyboard, not a steering wheel, just these two metallic-looking handprints set in a kind of dashboard. For a second he just sat there as strange symbols flickered on the monitor before him.

Outside, the pounding was getting louder. It sounded as if the aliens had traded in their hammers for a battering ram.

"*Now* would be a good time!" I shouted at Jack.

"No duh!" he shot back, tossing me a look over his shoulder. Then he turned back to the console. He was trying to look brave, but I could tell he was as nervous as I was. His forehead was sweating, his eyes darting frantically over the computer screen before him. He strummed his fingers—

And a low rumbling started somewhere deep in the bowels of the craft. It grew louder and louder until it was a constant humming, deeper and richer than anything I had ever heard before. The hammering outside stopped, replaced by shouts of anger as the aliens realized what we were doing. Then the humming turned into a high-pitched whine, and before I could say, *Maybe this isn't such a smart idea after all*, I felt the sudden lurch and rocking as the spaceship shot up off the ground!

The *g* force plastered us to the floor of the craft. I suddenly felt as if I weighed two tons.

Above us the domed ceiling became transparent, going from staticky white to clear. It was like looking up at the night sky from the inside of a fishbowl. All Ethan, Ashley, and I could do was stare up in awe as we shot up through the demolished roof of the mall, then straight up into a swirling funnel of glowing clouds that had formed over the reservoir. Soon we were hurtling through a corridor of beautiful golden light. *Is this what space looks like?* I wondered. Maybe we hadn't made it through liftoff after all, and this was the tunnel into the afterlife.

Then I saw Jack standing over me and realized that wherever I was, it wasn't heaven.

The *g* force had let up. Ethan and Ashley were already standing up.

Jack held out his hand to me.

"You did a pretty good job," I admitted grudgingly as Jack helped me to my feet. "I thought for sure we were going to crash into the ceiling. How did you manage to pilot it so smoothly?"

"Simple," he replied, grinning, "I just activated the program called 'Autopilot.'"

"You mean the ship is flying *itself?*" Ashley asked.

Jack nodded. "Uh-huh."

"You think that's a good idea?" I asked.

"Hey, it saved our butts, didn't it?" Jack said, his grin fading slightly.

"And exactly *what*," said Ethan, "are we supposed to do if the ship flies us right back to the aliens' planet?"

Jack's smile disappeared altogether. "I didn't think of that," he replied.

"Well, we better think of something—fast," I said, pointing toward the ceiling. "Look."

Outside, the light tunnel was widening to reveal the blue-green mass of a planet looming overhead. We were hurtling toward its surface at an enormous speed. As we approached, the ship slowly rotated until the planet was below us.

"How can we be here already?" I asked. "I thought it took years and years to travel to other planets."

"That strange tunnel . . . ," Ashley replied. "We must have been traveling through it at light speed or something. How else could we have gotten here so fast?"

"Perhaps it was a wormhole," Ethan answered, "a kind of doorway between two dimensions."

We were just entering the planet's atmosphere.

The craft shuddered as the planet's gravity seized hold of us.

"You know, there's something I've been meaning to ask you guys," Jack said in a troubled voice. "Something about the aliens. It's been bothering me, and I think I just figured it out now."

"What is it?" Ethan asked, his eyes glued to the ceiling. Below, outside the ship, the planet's surface came into view. The ship's monitors revealed a desolate, desert landscape swept by a harsh, dusty wind.

Jack continued, a little louder. "Don't you think it's weird that the aliens were speaking English? I mean, it's not just when they're pretending to be human but when they speak to each *other*, too. And then there's their *written* language . . ."

He gestured at the computer monitors, which were filled with a bunch of weird, unintelligible symbols. "I mean, it *looks* like gobbledygook, but—"

"Hey, look," Ashley interrupted, as a large crater-covered orb hovered into view on the overhead screen. "They have a moon just like ours."

"You're not letting me finish!" Jack shouted. "These alien symbols. They're like a combination of different languages . . . different *Earth* languages."

"What are you saying, Jack?" I asked.

"What I'm saying is, that doesn't just *look* like

our moon," Jack said, pointing. "It *is* our moon."

"What?" we all said, equally shocked.

"But that would mean . . ." I let the sentence die on my lips.

With a slight wobble on its six spindly legs, the alien craft touched down, settled on the ground.

Wordlessly we headed to the hatchway.

With a feeling of dread, I ran my hand over the switch.

The doors hissed open. The gangway lowered. The air that rushed in, though foul smelling, was still breathable. The four of us descended, single file, then stood side by side, squinting at the impossible sight before us.

We were surrounded by a wasteland. Crumbled rock and rubble stretching as far as the eye could see. The ground was pockmarked and barren, without a single sign of life.

In the distance small, pitiful fires burned, sending columns of inky smoke into a polluted yellow sky.

"There's no *way* this is Earth," Ethan whispered. "No way . . ."

Then Ashley gasped. She pointed. And we saw it.

A single, broken letter *M* was sticking halfway out of the charred soil.

The large bronze letter had tarnished, corroding partially away. It looked like the ancient relic of some long dead civilization. Not one of the Ms that had once hung on the side of the Metier Mall.

But that's what it was.

"It's a time machine," Jack replied somberly. "The UFO isn't a spaceship; it's a time machine. And *this* . . . this is Earth's future."

No single vocabulary word could describe how I felt at that very moment. But as I stared out over the devastated ruins in front of me a million different questions flooded my brain:

How had this happened?

When had this happened?

Who had caused it?

And then a question came back to me that had never really left:

Can we alter our destiny?

Or is the future set in stone, unchangeable?

I had a feeling that the four of us were going to find out.

About the Author

Chris Archer grew up in New Jersey, where he spent most of his childhood wishing he had special powers.

He now divides his time between New York City and Los Angeles, California. When Chris is not writing books and screenplays, he enjoys going to scary movies, playing piano (badly), and reading suspense novels.

He has never been to Wisconsin.

Don't miss

Flash Forward

Coming in mid-July
From MINSTREL Paperbacks